Love is
a time of enchantment:
in it all days are fair and all fields
green. Youth is blest by it,
old age made benign:
the eyes of love see
roses blooming in December,
and sunshine through rain. Verily
is the time of true-love
a time of enchantment — and
Oh! how eager is woman
to be bewitched!

A COURT FOR OWLS

After her father's death, Jane Terrill finds herself part owner of extensive Australian property, and with her uncle and aunt, the co-heirs, she travels to Australia. On the way, she befriends two children and their widowed father, Simon Sandford. A remarkable chance saves Jane from the disaster which overtakes her aunt and uncle, and she settles on her estates with Simon. But her happiness is soon under threat. In the end, her own life is at stake, and she has to find the truth about others — and herself.

Books by Nara Lake
in the Ulverscroft Large Print Series:

THE PAINTED GIRL
THE TRAITOR HEART

NARA LAKE

A COURT
FOR OWLS

Complete and Unabridged

ULVERSCROFT
Leicester

First published in Great Britain

First Large Print Edition
published 1996

British Library CIP Data

Lake, Nara
A court for owls.—Large print ed.—
Ulverscroft large print series: romance
I. Title
823.914 [F]

ISBN 0–7089–3450–1

Published by
F. A. Thorpe (Publishing) Ltd.
Anstey, Leicestershire

Set by Words & Graphics Ltd.
Anstey, Leicestershire
Printed and bound in Great Britain by
T. J. Press (Padstow) Ltd., Padstow, Cornwall

This book is printed on acid-free paper

1

IN retrospect, it was strange that the day upon which she had last seen Evan Whiteside was also the one when she had first met Simon Sandford, although she had been unaware of the latter's identity then, and indeed, had barely noticed him as a person.

Too much had happened recently. Her father had died just as a new and wonderful life had opened up for both of them. She had met her Aunt Dorcas, only sister of her own mother, for the first time, and Dorcas's husband Hugh MacBride, always to be remembered as dear Uncle Hugh.

The MacBrides had come to the inexpensive but respectable Bristol inn in response to her own telegram, leaving their junior children in the care of relatives at Bath. The three elder boys had already been settled at school, this task being in part the MacBrides' reason for a long voyage to England from outlandish

New South Wales.

Jane Terrill and her father had arrived a few days too early for the planned meeting with the MacBrides, and the Reverend Peregrine Terrill had succumbed to the heart condition which had troubled him for several years. This time there would be no recovery: he passed away a few minutes before Mr. and Mrs. MacBride arrived.

He knew that he was dying, and as he fought for breath, he told her that she must enter her new life with a cheerful heart, and a faith that all would be well from now on. Jane had wept, and had cried out that it was so wrong that he should leave her now that their troubles were almost over.

"No, child, it was not to be." His words came out in sobbing gasps as he struggled against the pain and the deadly congestion in his collapsed lungs. "Remember Lot's wife, my dearest and best of daughters. Never look back. All I ask, Jenny, is that sometimes you remember that it was I who in the end led you to the Promised Land."

"Oh, Papa!" In spite of her tears, Jane

could not help wondering at the way in which he tore out these last few sentences from his dying body. "Don't leave me alone!" She held him close to her, and even as she did this, he stiffened in her arms.

"Oh, God, my Heavenly Father, prepare to receive Thy humble and penitent son, for I am going the way of all the earth."

The doctor moved from his place at the foot of the bed and gently disengaged Jane's arms from her father's slight shoulders. He laid the Reverend Terrill back on his pillows, shook his head, and turned to the young woman.

"He's gone, Miss Terrill, and may his Maker receive him as he wished."

Death was a daily phenomenon to the doctor, for much of his work was in the poorest back streets of Bristol, but his voice was gruff with emotion. The Reverend Terrill's white hair, worn a little longer than was fashionable, the gentle blue eyes now closed forever, and the finely boned features had, at the last, a radiance about them which reminded that pragmatic practitioner of some murals he had once seen, a long time ago, as a youth touring Italy. Raphael, he thought was the artist, and even as a lad still in his teens, he had marvelled at the delicacy and beauty of the saints' faces, wondering where on this wicked earth there could have been found such models amidst venal human beings.

Jane Terrill stared at him as if she did not comprehend. She was, thought the doctor, exactly what one always expected a parson's daughter to be. In her early twenties, she was a mousy little thing, quietly and dowdily dressed in an unflattering brown gown which made her complexion almost sallow, and effectively camouflaged the fact that the body beneath the tucked, high-necked bodice and very modestly wide skirts was small-waisted and nicely curved in the right places. Also, the hands which were now clasped together in grief were small, slim-fingered, and well-kept, with rosily buffed nails. Miss Terrill, it appeared, was not without her small vanities.

"You have other family?" asked the doctor, kindly, closing his bag after scrawling out the death certificate.

She nodded.

"Yes. I am expecting them hourly. I had a telegram telling me that they were coming at noon."

As if on cue, there was a tap on the door, and the doctor opened it to reveal the landlord's wife. Her mouth opened into an 'O' as she glimpsed the still man on the bed.

"He's gone?" she exclaimed, and then became businesslike. "I trust you'll make arrangements immediately. Other guests don't like there bein' a corpse on the premises."

"I'll speak to the undertaker on my way home," promised the doctor, preparing to leave.

"Well, what I come up to say was there's company for Miss Terrill down below in the parlour," said the woman, and there was something like a grudging respect in her voice.

From the first, she had not been pleased by the arrival of the ailing parson and his quiet, almost shabby, daughter. She had an instinct about thin purses, and long experience had taught her to identify the signs of

5

failing life. The Reverend Mr. Terrill had a transparency about his skin which she had distrusted, and left to herself, she would have turned away the couple with their pitifully small amount of luggage and the unmistakable aura of shabby-genteel. However, her husband was softer-hearted, and he had allotted them the two cheapest, and smallest, rooms after the girl had explained that they had a very important appointment here in Bristol. The landlord had gathered that there was money involved in this appointment, but his wife had scoffed, and when the clergyman had collapsed that very night, her attitude was one of 'told you so'.

Now it appeared that this tale about the important appointment had been true all along. The man and woman downstairs, although colonial, were obviously wealthy, and had looked about them in the parlour with something very near contempt.

Jane hesitated. She did not wish yet to leave her father, but there was nothing else she could do.

"Be so good as to tell them that I shall be down presently," she said, in a crisp little voice which had in it just a hint of a tremor.

In her own small room, she tidied her brown hair, rinsed her tear-stained face in cold water, and stared anxiously at her reflection in the looking-glass. This was to be the most important moment of her life. Would they accept her as part heiress to a large fortune?

Her father, who must have been aware for some time that his life was running out, had drilled her well, assuring her that all the papers he had forwarded after reading that advertisement in *The Times* were correct and in absolute order. If she answered all questions as he had instructed her, he said, she would have nothing to worry about.

For Jane, life was beginning. She would start a new existence in another country, she must marry if the opportunity presented itself, have her own family, and forget all the miseries and uncertainties which had gone before.

"Do not forget," he had whispered to her before the doctor came, and after the clergyman he had requested to minister last rites had left. "Do exactly as I have told you, and be of good heart always. I die knowing that I have given you as much as a father can give."

She must not mourn, she had been told, only take full advantage of the wonderful chance which had come her way. He had done his part. Now, it was up to her.

But what if they did not accept her? It was feasible that Mrs. MacBride, at least, would resent the way in which her own father had undergone a change of heart and had included Jane Terrill in his will.

It was too late for misgivings. Jane took a deep breath to steady herself, and went downstairs.

The parlour was tiny and chilly, for the fire flickering in the grate had been alight only a few minutes, in honour of the wealthy visitors. The inconvenience of sheltering a shabby and sick clergyman and his dowdy daughter was forgotten and forgiven, and the landlord's wife, all politeness and smiles, offered tea, which was quietly declined.

Mrs. MacBride, Aunt Dorcas, was an imposing woman of thirty seven years, expensively dressed in heavy dark green corded silk, topped by a short fur mantlet, which in turn was matched by her fur-trimmed bonnet. Like many well-to-do matrons of her era, she carried too much weight, which was emphasised by her heavy clothing. In spite of this, she complained incessantly about the cold English spring, this being a custom, Jane discovered later, amongst visitors from the Antipodes.

However, she was overall a handsome woman, with splendid auburn hair, strongly formed facial features, proud brown eyes, and it had to be admitted, absolutely no physical resemblance to Miss Jane Terrill.

This last featured in what was Mrs. MacBride's first remark after preliminary self-introductions.

"Well, you're certainly not like your mother," she said, taking in Jane critically, and no doubt assessing the exact cost of every stitch worn by the girl. She turned to her husband, a stoutish, somewhat florid, but amiable-looking man in his middle forties, who was warming large, square hands before the struggling fire.

"You did not meet my sister!" she said to him, almost accusingly.

"No, m'dear. We did not meet until after her death," he responded, mildly.

"You must take after your father's family," continued Mrs. MacBride, turning back to Jane.

"I believe that is so," murmured Jane. Her damp handkerchief was screwed tightly into her left palm. "You know that my father died only . . . only twenty minutes ago."

Dorcas MacBride's gloved hand flew to her mouth. She was shocked, but at the same time another expression briefly changed her face before she brought it under the proper, solemn control. Was it relief?

"We did not know. The landlady did not mention it."

Hugh MacBride was not perhaps quite top drawer by English standards, but he possessed a ready sympathy when It was needed. "I am so sorry. What can I do to help?"

His kindness was too much. Jane's attempt at self-control collapsed into bitter tears.

Yet, in the following days, there was little time for prolonged grief. Jane's new-found connections were at the end of their European tour. MacBride, of Scots extraction, but Australian born, had satisfied his curiosity about his father's native land. Now, he was preparing to return to his Sydney business and the management of his New South Wales properties. He was a wealthy man in his own right, and it did not matter to him that his wife's inheritance from her ship-owner, sheep-run entrepreneur, colliery-magnate father was lessened by the old man's decision to include his long-lost grand-daughter Jane in the dispersal of his estate.

Horatio Wilson had fathered only two children, both girls, in a late marriage, and his older daughter, Emily, had been intended as wife for another colonial magnate. At the last moment, with all the wedding preparations made, she had eloped with a poor English curate who had just arrived in Sydney. Emily had not been forgiven, and when she had died from cholera two years later, there had been no attempt made to claim the infant Jane as one of his family.

Wilson's change of mind so late in life had both astounded and irked his surviving child, Dorcas. She had been fruitful during her married life, now having seven children, four sons and three daughters. Although MacBride was no pauper, she had counted on receiving the whole of her father's wealth to set them up — and any future offspring — in the style she felt they deserved.

However, to do Mrs. MacBride credit, she was a fair-minded and kindly woman, willing to overcome her prejudice against this young kinswoman who had been living in what appeared to be very meagre circumstances. The solicitor who had been entrusted with the task of seeking out the missing heiress had explained to the MacBrides that the Reverend Peregrine Terrill had been forced by chronic ill-health into retirement on a very modest income.

Remembering her father's intense dislike of his unwanted son-in-law, Mrs. MacBride could only wonder at the marvellous ways of Providence. It was, well, fortunate that she would not have to be pleasant to the man who had caused her sister's defection. These days, she had to stretch her memory to recollect what Peregrine had looked like. He had been a slight, insignificant person, but with a puckish humour and quick wit which had enchanted lively, pretty Emily, who had been so bored by dull Sydney society.

Both MacBrides expected that Jane would prefer to remain in civilised England to enjoy her considerable income, and they were taken aback to hear that she intended to travel to Australia 'to see things for myself'. They, Hugh MacBride pointed out, had roots out there, and were prepared to overlook shortcomings, but she would find the climate tiresome and the society commonplace. She would do far better to remain in Britain, find herself a nice little place, and live in the manner suitable to a young lady of means.

No, her mind was made up. The solicitor had mentioned a country estate called Curwood, about seventy miles out of Melbourne, in the colony of Victoria. This appeared to have been left to her in its entirety. She was not of a nature to sit back idly.

"Good heavens, Curwood ain't a nice little country estate. It's a sheep and cattle run. Given there's a house on the homestead block, but the bush ain't the place for a gentlewoman. By the Lord Harry, the country all about has been turned upside down by the gold rush. The diggers can go anywhere they fancy on land belonging to the Crown, and Curwood is mostly leased from the Crown, excepting a few hundred acres that make up the homestead block."

"Well, I'm sure that a few hundred acres are enough."

"Not in Australia, they ain't."

With this, Hugh MacBride gave up. Let the girl find out for herself. He put her obduracy down to romantic fancies, influenced probably by those apocryphal illustrations of Australian life which appeared in the magazines. These depicted leafy glades inhabited by elegant young men clad casually in a sort of Italian bandit outfit, awaiting News from Home. No dirt was visible, and neither were snakes, flies, itinerant 'old lags' who had not bathed in two years, meat going off in hot weather, nor stacks of

14

empty bottles lying about squalid huts or tattered tents.

His wife, Jane's aunt, was not particularly pleased, either, but she had to admit that the children, now arrived from Bath, had taken immediately to their new relative. Mrs MacBride would have been an abnormal mother if she had not faced with trepidation the prospect of thirteen thousand miles by sea with her four lively young children on board. She employed a personal maid as well as a nursery governess, both of whom would be returning to Sydney with the family, but anyone else who would take some of the brunt suddenly acquired merit. From experience, she knew how her husband coped with a sea voyage. He would find kindred souls amidst the other male passengers and play cards. He did not play for high stakes. He simply retreated into a world of diamonds, clubs, hearts and spades, smoking too much, and filling in the occasional interval with dull talk about wool prices, the independence of the Australian working class, and so forth.

2

SO it was that, after initial opposition, Hugh MacBride booked the extra passage needed for Miss Terrill. The family was to travel on the crack, Clyde-built clipper, *Kincardine*, due to be cleared out of Bristol as soon as loading was finished.

The reason for MacBride's choice in this year of 1857 when a possibly quicker passage would have been available on a steam and sail vessel was that the *Kincardine*, on this particular voyage out, was carrying only first and cabin class passengers. Eastern Australia was flourishing with the wealth from the great gold discoveries, and the ship's owners decided that a carefully selected cargo could be more profitable than a hold full of steerage immigrants. There were plenty of rich Australians happy to pay extra for the comfort of a large ship and a short passenger list on the outward run, as a touch of luxury at the end of their

British and European holidays.

Over the past few years, conditions on the twelve thousand mile voyage to Australia had improved dramatically. The sailing ship, reaching its ultimate development, was still able to hold its own against steamers, for it was not fettered to the necessity of long and dirty stops at coaling stations. Nevertheless, the prudent passenger investigated his or her accommodation beforehand, and although cabins were sybaritic compared with those of former times, the addition of a shelf for books and oddments, extra hooks for clothes, and so forth, could be necessary and was not frowned upon by the owners.

Then there was diet to be considered. The best ships advertised that they carried hens for fresh eggs (and as they stopped laying towards the end of the voyage, poultry meals), and an assortment of beasts to provide milk and fresh meat. Of course, the intending passenger could not reasonably expect all his or her tastes to be satisfied, and a tuck box of extras such as raisins, apples and dainty biscuit — and seidlitz powder to offset that inevitable 'Travellers' complaint' — was a part of cabin luggage.

More frightening in those days of improved travel than the possibility of storms and shipwreck was the spectre of boredom during three or four months out of sight of land. Ladies could take their embroidery (although if they had children on board, women had their hands full enough), and both sexes needed plenty of reading matter, as well as day books, sketch pads, and note paper upon which to record anything of interest.

Having gained her way and obeyed her father's injunction to start a fresh life, Jane Terrill prepared energetically for the voyage. Mr. MacBride arranged for an advance of money, and with the limited time left to her, after arranging for a suitable headstone on her father's grave, she shopped widely, but carefully. Her wardrobe had been very small, and much patched and made over. The wearing of mourning did not mean that she had to hide herself under dowdy and out-of-date styles, insisted Aunt Dorcas. The garments stitched up so quickly by a dressmaker and her assistants were well cut and in the modes of the latest fashion plates. Aunt Dorcas warned Jane that all styles in Australia had to be at least one season behind, and summer dresses made now for her post mourning period would still be the height of fashion for two years in Sydney. Therefore, what seemed to be extravagance was, in fact, thrift.

Bonnets, gloves, shawls, boots, underwear, night attire — the list seemed endless and the amount of money spent astronomical. Newly and smartly attired, Jane thought to throw out her old clothes, but a young maid at the fashionable hotel where the MacBrides were staying begged for them. They would be gratefully used by her mother, the girl said, for cutting down into clothes for the young 'uns.

"Please take them."

Jane turned quickly away to hide the tears springing to her eyes. As if he were there in the room, she could hear Papa saying, in that quiet, but so beautifully modulated voice, the old, old words.

"Blessed is he that considereth the poor: the Lord will deliver him in time of trouble."

How quickly one adapted to better

19

circumstances! Already, the years she had spent with Papa were fading backwards, rather like the scenery when one travelled by train. One did not really forget, but it was no longer there. Affluence, she was discovering, enveloped one so utterly. Yet, all this was obeying Papa's deathbed wishes, the moving forward and upward, changing from the poor mouse of a retired parson's daughter to a young woman of means. If only it had come earlier . . .

That same day, there would be a more drastic reminder of the past than a young chambermaid begging for cast-off clothes. She was in a bookshop when it happened. Aunt Dorcas did not approve of her going out on her own, even in this best, respectable part of the old seaport city, for Mrs. MacBride did not quite understand how poverty makes one self-reliant and unused to such appendages as chaperones. Still, Aunt Dorcas was very busy as the hour for embarkation drew near, and the bookshop was only a few doors and past a corner from the hotel.

Jane enjoyed reading, and she intended to make the most of the voyage by wallowing in novels. Papa, too, had been an enthusiastic reader, although more inclined to serious and philosophical works, and frequently, he had reprimanded his daughter about her fondness for entertaining rather than improving books. At the young ladies' academy where she had boarded until she was past eighteen, fiction had been regarded as a work of the devil, and she could still recall, with a shudder, the furore when several pupils, including herself, had been caught sighing over the wild and improbable 'Wuthering Heights'. Come to think of it, she had never finished reading 'Wuthering Heights'.

There was a copy on the shelf in front of her, so she added it to the volumes of Tennyson and Byron she had already chosen. Ah, and there was Mrs. Gaskell's 'Mary Barton'. That was another novel she had not finished reading. It had been inadvertently left behind during one of their moves.

It stood to reason that other passengers on the *Kincardine* would have their own selections of books, and with the possibility of exchanges, there was no point in buying too much. But a selection of the works of Mr. Charles Dickens, tempted her. She had missed out on the last two of the monthly parts of 'Hard Times' when they had moved to Ostend, and she was picking up the complete volume when it happened.

"Why, Miss Jane — ah — the surname — Terrill?" purred a masculine voice in her ear, and paling with a sickly realisation, she slowly turned, the book still in her black-gloved hand.

"I do not wish to speak with you," she whispered. Please go away."

Evan Whiteside chuckled.

"Ah, Jenny, at least allow me to offer my condolences," he sneered, taking the volume from her limp hand and glancing at the spine. "'Hard Times'? We know all about that, don't we?"

"All right, you've offered your condolences, and I've accepted. Now please go."

Her slight form had stiffened, and she bit her lower lip as she attempted to retain an illusion of aloof dignity. At the same time, she studied the man surreptitiously. He was, she believed, about thirty years of age, nicely barbered in a style reminiscent of the better cavalry regiments, one of which had actually seen his services during the Crimean war. He liked to give the impression that he had been commissioned, but Papa had been reasonably sure that he had served in a fairly humble capacity.

Evan Whiteside was a well-built man, not too handsome, but fresh complexioned with wide apart, oddly guileless, blue eyes. Superficially, he was very smartly dressed in London man-about-town style, even to the long overcoat affected by the 'heavy swells', but close and shrewd inspection gave a distinct impression of the second-hand shop and cheap copying. He was not in the least discouraged by her abruptness, but came closer, and stooped slightly so that she could hear his softly spoken words.

Papa, of course, had the appropriate quote from Holy Writ to describe this dreadful man. "'The words of his mouth were smoother than butter, but war was in his heart'." Ugh!

"I learned that you had come to Bristol, and traced you to a certain small back street inn. And what a tale mine host had to tell — the poor, sick, old parson and his devoted daughter, taken in only out of pure compassion with scant hope that the score could be paid. Then, the miracle — rich colonial relatives arriving out of the blue to rescue the grieving orphan. Ah, Jenny, what a strange old world it is."

"Let poor Papa rest in the peace he so richly deserves, and be so good as to leave me alone!"

"My dear girl, you sound exactly like the heroine of a play — a very bad play — I attended last night." His voice lost its bantering note and hardened. "Your father's death isn't the end of it."

As he spoke, he produced a couple of sovereigns, and handed them to the hovering bookshop owner, who was all obsequiousness.

"I can pay for my own books, thank you," hissed Jane, as the owner hurried away to wrap the purchases.

"From what I was told at the inn, I'm sure you can," replied Whiteside, imperturbably. "Let us say that I'm priming the pump. Do you wish the purchases to be sent to your present address?"

She saw immediately through this ploy. So, he did not know where she was lodging. When the MacBrides had arrived so hastily just after Papa's death, they had not yet made arrangements for their stay in Bristol, and by sheer luck, the establishment they had first chosen had been unable to accommodate the enlarged party. This confusion must have misled Whiteside, and it was sheer ill fortune which had allowed him to glimpse her entering the shop. So, as Papa had always said, when merciful Providence showed the way, it was up to us poor mortals to follow it.

"I wish to take them with me!"

The bookshop proprietor looked just a little surprised and suspicious. Well dressed ladies were not supposed to be seen carrying parcels, there was no sign of a carriage and attendant flunkey outside, and this man who had paid for the books had something about him . . . he was not quality.

"And I shall carry them," smiled Whiteside, very sure of himself.

Once outside the store, she turned right instead of left, walking briskly away from her hotel, awaiting her opportunity. She was sorry about the books, but seeing that he had paid for them, he could keep them.

"Oh!" she declared, stopping suddenly and looking back. "I've dropped my handkerchief."

He too stopped and looked back, sighting the scrap of black-edged cambric some twenty feet behind. Keeping up the pose of protective gentleman, he retraced his steps, and then, as he stooped, she darted across the busy intersection, risking life and limb in the confusion of horses and vehicles. The driver of a heavy wagon yelled at her in a thick Irish brogue as she missed being trampled by mere inches, and then a hand grabbed her arm and jerked her to the safety of the narrow footpath.

"That was a stupid thing to do," a male voice reprimanded her.

She saw Whiteside on the other side of the street, poised for the chance to follow her, and she made a desperate decision.

"That well-dressed man is annoying

me," she said, in a low tone. "Would it be possible for you to escort me to the end of the street where I can hire a hansom to take me to my lodgings? And, please, could you act as if you know me?"

He did appear startled, but the small, pale face under the modish black bonnet was imploring. Gallantly, he placed his hand under her elbow just like a bona-fide acquaintance would.

Whiteside changed his mind about following her, and after staring ferociously across the street, turned, and strode away.

"An unwanted suitor?" queried the stranger, who, as well he might, appeared to be rather interested.

"A mere acquaintance. He forced himself upon my notice whilst I was in the bookshop." Her voice trembled, quite genuinely. "Thank you so very much for your assistance."

"My pleasure," he said, curtly, making it plain that he had no wish to become further involved. Obligingly, he hailed a passing hansom and handed her in, touching the brim of his tall hat before moving away.

She watched him for a moment before sinking back with a sigh. He was a tall man, not at all bad looking, but with a sombre, almost brooding, cast of expression. My guardian angel must have sent him, she thought, and felt a great relief that this evening she would be safely on board the *Kincardine*.

3

SETTLING on board the fine clipper *Kincardine* took some time. The MacBrides had their three small daughters and youngest boy (very crestfallen at leaving his elder brothers behind in their school) to sort out into the appropriate quarters, together with a ladies' maid and a nursery governess. Naturally, as an addition to the group, Jane Terrill was drawn into the muddle which was still only partly unravelled at nightfall and sailing time.

She was secretly thankful that she was thus occupied, and excused herself from staying on deck to watch the preparations for departure with the less encumbered passengers. Her meeting with Evan Whiteside, that unpleasant reminder of the past, had unnerved her, and even as busy tugs pulled the *Kincardine* out into the Bristol Channel, she knew that she would not feel really secure until the vessel was well past Land's End.

Yet, in the morning, as she joined others for that last glimpse of Cornwall's rocky shores, it was as much as she could do not to weep. She could never return. She knew that she had every reason for wanting to leave England, but with the brisk wind filling the *Kincardine*'s great sails and the coastline receding rapidly, her throat was choked with tears. Reason told her that to follow her father's advice and start a new life was the only course to take, but already she was miserably homesick.

The greater number of persons on the passenger list on this voyage were Australians, born or by adoption, and as they were mostly wealthy merchants or graziers, their remarks were a mixture of sorrow to be leaving the comforts of a civilised country and gladness to be on the way home.

"Holiday's over," said one grizzled pioneer who had obviously made good. "Now it's time to think of gettin' back to work."

"I'll miss our grandchildren," said his wife, wistfully, before brightening, "but I'll be glad to be in my own home again.

I do hope my garden has been cared for properly while we've been away."

Separated from Jane by two solid bodies, a man was lifting a small boy of about three on to his shoulders, the better for the child to see the lighthouse beyond Land's End. A small girl at his coat-tails was demanding her turn in a shrill voice, and Jane forgot her sadness as, with a decided shock, she recognised the man as her 'guardian angel' of the previous morning.

Hurriedly, she left the deck, and retreated to the cabin she was sharing with ten year old Alice, the eldest MacBride girl. The last thing she wanted was for the MacBrides to learn about her encounter with Evan Whiteside. To cover up the fruitlessness of her expedition to buy books, she had paid a bootboy a small sum to go out and purchase those same volumes — or their duplicates — which she supposed Whiteside to have still in his possession. There was a touch of irony in this last, for she knew that Whiteside, in spite of his carefully cultivated veneer, was certainly not given to any of the more cultural pursuits.

In the temporary safety of the cabin, she had to review, in a calm and rational manner, the unfortunate chance of her rescuer being on board. Take a few deep breaths, she told herself, sit down, and think it out. Things are never as bad as they seem. That was Papa's favourite axiom.

Fact one. It was no use hoping that the man would not recognise her. In deep mourning, she could not even attempt a disguise by changing the colour of her costume.

Fact two. He had with him two small children. The rather objectionable little girl with the shrill voice had called him Father. Somewhere, there was a mother. Wives encumbered by small children did not like their husbands talking to young single girls, even ones as colourless and innocuous as Jane Terrill.

Fact three. If Aunt Dorcas heard about it, she would ask questions, and questions, and questions. Aunt Dorcas was like that. She would appear to be quite satisfied, and then out of the blue, she would make another of her pointed queries.

The problem was laid aside for the next three days. As the ship moved out into the wide stretches of the Atlantic, the weather worsened to an extent that most of the passengers preferred to remain in their cabins, being in many cases too ill to struggle to the dining saloon where everything not nailed or screwed down moved about alarmingly.

When this stretch was behind them, and the *Kincardine* was speeding southwards gracefully and steadily with a strong, but not boisterous, following wind, most passengers revived as if a magic wand had been waved. Travellers took their constitutionals about the deck, the men looking up and about and conversing with the ship's officers in what they all hoped was a knowledgeable and not too land-lubberish way, whilst the ladies promenaded in the light clothes they had been advised to bring for travel through the warmer regions. Truth to tell, the breeze was still chilly, and most were glad to wrap themselves in shawls before long, but the sunshine promised better things to come.

Jane kept an eye open for her rescuer,

and dodged him successfully until the midday meal. For the first time, there was a full sitting, and Jane found herself seated diagonally opposite him at the one long table in the dining saloon. He was placed between a returning Sydney banker and a good-looking woman in her late twenties. This woman, Jane had already learnt, was a certain Mrs. O'Brien, a wealthy widow returning to southern Australia after a prolonged tour undertaken to help her over the loss of Mr. O'Brien.

She had a roving glance and a ready laugh, and Jane suspected that she wore rouge, as well as brilliantining her hair into a glossy smoothness.

"The type of woman," Papa would have said, "who thinks that one can hide one's vulgar origins by smothering oneself under silk."

As an aid to sociability, the passengers at each of the two sittings had been seated so that they were not next to spouses or relatives, and Jane was thus separated from Uncle Hugh (as she now called him) by a very boring colonial politician and a stout female who spent her time

34

between mouthfuls glaring disapprovingly at the flirtatious Mrs. O'Brien.

"Why, Simon Sandford!" Uncle Hugh's voice boomed out across the table. "Didn't know you were on board. Where've you been hiding."

Disaster, thought Jane. They know one another.

"I haven't. The children's governess has been seasick ever since we sailed, poor soul, and I'm playing nursemaid. Fortunately, the stewardess is seeing to their meals."

As he spoke, his sombre eyes passed briefly over Jane, and besides fright, she felt another, very different emotion.

He was about thirty, well set up without being too heavy, and as she had observed earlier, he was quite handsome, if one excepted a rather jutting nose. He had very black hair, neatly styled, and matching black mutton chop whiskers, and eyes which, although she had thought them at first to be black, were in fact grey and deepset under dark but finely shaped brows. His skin was very pale, almost colourless, and his lips thin but not too much so. His hands were large and well-shaped, and he wore a heavy signet ring on the left middle finger. In a time when jewellery for men, except watch-chains and necktie pins, was out of style, this seemed affected in contrast to his dark garb. There was about him that sombreness which she had noticed at their first encounter, an almost brooding aspect of sadness.

Nothing could have been more designed to upset Jane's good sense. During the past few days, being a good sailor and bereft of company because of the seasickness which had afflicted so many others, she had finally finished reading 'Wuthering Heights' after a lapse of several years. It had proved to be even more stirring than she remembered from the time when an indignant headmistress had confiscated the copy being passed from one fourteen-year-old to another. Heathcliffe, she decided as she regretfully closed the covers after the last words had been feverishly consumed, was even more romantic than that other ideal of fiction, Mr. Rochester.

For a quite considerable period, she had longed to become a governess, preferably in a gloomy and ramshackle mansion miles from anywhere, in the faint hope of finding herself in the clutches of a Mr. Edward Rochester. Jane could cope with the Evan Whitesides of this world: faced by a passably good-looking man of brunet colouring and a tragic aspect and she became prey to the most ridiculous dreams. Well, Jane Eyre in the Bronte romance had been plain and small and ordinary, had she not?

Come down to earth, she told herself sternly. Mrs. Sandford, no doubt, has also been a victim of *mal de mer* and is not yet sufficiently strong to join us at the table.

The brooding eyes still rested on her, thoughtfully, and with presence of mind, she kept her face straight and her expression remotely polite, presenting the very epitome of a reserved young lady who would not dream of speaking to a man until they were properly introduced. Sandford appeared puzzled, and then Mrs. O'Brien, quick to stop his attention going elsewhere, spoke in her penetrating voice.

How difficult for him on such a long

voyage with two young children and a sick governess!

"I'm sure she'll be well tomorrow," said the man, firmly, and at that moment, the boring politician began explaining the tedious ins and outs of New South Wales land laws to Jane, and she could do nothing but listen.

Now, Mrs. MacBride, her children's governess and Jane had already arranged to share the task of taking the children at lessons. Little Charlton MacBride, being only four, was exempted from more formal instruction, but he was already shaping his letters, and Jane, because she was considered too inexperienced to cope with the older children, found herself in charge of the little boy whilst the others, unwillingly, bent their heads over their lessons. Work for the slate over for the day, she yielded to his demands for a story, and before long, discovered that she had two additions to her audience, the children of Mr. Sandford.

As soon as the story ended, Charlton was eager to be off playing with his new friends, but the little girl lingered. Unlike her brother, who was fair, she had inherited her father's raven hair.

"My name's Dorothy Sandford," she announced, in a slightly superior voice, "and this is my little brother, Rodney."

At this instant, Sandford arrived, a little flustered.

"Oh, there you are," he said, and then stared down at Jane, who was still seated in her sheltered spot out of the breeze. "I'm sorry if they've forced themselves on you, Miss . . . ?"

"Terrill," she said quietly, whilst her heart thumped. "Please don't scold them. I was telling a story, and they stopped to listen. I find that rather flattering."

"I'm not much good at that sort of thing."

"I shall most likely be telling Charlton a story each afternoon. He is still a little young for formal lessons."

"Do you mean to say that you can make up a fresh story each time?" He was frowning now, as if not believing her.

"Mr. Sandford, I'm by no means as clever as all that. I adapt stories I've read or have been told."

All this time, as she spoke, she treated him as a stranger.

"Then, if my children are not a nuisance, may they join young Master MacBride?"

"Of course!" She gathered up her courage. "Mr. Sandford, may I fling myself upon your mercy?"

Was it her imagination, or did a flash of amusement briefly illuminate those sombre eyes?

"I think I understand. Miss Terrill, it is obvious to me that you wish me to forget our first meeting. I shall oblige you."

Then, he gathered his children and went on his way, whilst Jane sat very still, almost numb with relief.

After the initial adjustment, the passengers settled down to passing the time of the voyage, which was expected to last something between twelve and sixteen weeks, depending on favourable winds. It was planned that the *Kincardine* would sail almost due south to the fortieth parallel of latitude. From then on, borne along at a great rate by the blustering Roaring Forties gales, it would be 'eastering' until a point southwest of Adelaide in South Australia was reached. The ship would then commence the last part of the voyage, which was often the most perilous, for Australia's southern coastline was wild, sparsely inhabited, and already had claimed many lives in fearful shipwrecks. The approach to Melbourne in Victoria was notorious, for in the Bass Straits between the Australian mainland and island Tasmania, the weather changed for the worse almost without warning.

This, of course, was several weeks ahead, and for a while, before plunging into the storms of the southern winter, the passengers of the *Kincardine* would enjoy the warmth of the tropics and such nonsense as King Neptune's visit when the ship 'crossed the line'. Whilst the weather remained fine, and the ship reasonably steady, various ways of passing the time were organised.

A ship's newspaper was compiled and printed on a small hand press. It contained minor items of gossip, the account of sighting a school of porpoises, the passing of a man-o'-war, a not very relevant piece about the horrors of Balaclava copied from someone's magazine, and some terrible poetry

41

composed by A Gentlewoman On Board. You should write down one of your stories so we can print it in the next issue," said Mr. Sandford to Miss Terrill one hot afternoon as the ship made very slow progress with a slack following breeze.

"I . . . " She paused in the middle of a refusal. She had less confidence in her prowess with the pen than in the art of direct story telling, but she wanted very badly to attract his favourable notice.

"Please do. After all, Mrs. O'Brien has obliged us with a poem."

So! Mrs. O'Brien was A Gentlewoman On Board.

How Jane loathed Mrs. O'Brien with her carrying laugh, her ready repartee, and her magnificent figure shown off so well in this hot climate by low-necked, too frilly, too youthful, dresses. Most of all, and somewhat unfairly, Jane hated her because the widow was no longer tied to circumspect behaviour by a state of mourning. It was not proper to dance whilst wearing black. Jane did not begrudge poor Papa a few weeks out of her life, but to sit out whilst

Mr. Sandford danced the polka with the flashy Mrs. O'Brien was almost too much to bear. Afterwards, Mrs. O'Brien invariably declared that she was so hot that she must stroll a while about the deck. Just as invariably, Mr. Sandford accompanied her.

Mr. Sandford was not the only unattached man amongst the passengers. There was one in particular, the son of that boring New South Wales politician, who made it clear that he liked Jane's company, and in this he was encouraged by Uncle Hugh MacBride. He was a thoroughly nice young man, but Jane was in the grips of her first and most agonising love.

Now, when Sandford had made his request about the story, she wished to prolong his interest.

"I shall try," she said, shyly, "but I'm no authoress."

"You don't take after your father?"

The question surprised her, but he admitted that Hugh MacBride had informed him that Jane's father had supported them both by his pen for a number of years.

"I don't know. I've never tried."

"Well, now's your chance."

He and another man had been elected to the task of bringing out the ship's newspaper. As so often happens in such circumstances, creative enthusiasm had died early, and Sandford was having to resort to persuasion and mild bullying to obtain contributions.

She knew that he saw her only as the plain, quiet, reliable young lady who could be found most afternoons with an interested audience of small fry. She was someone to be taken for granted. Miss Lark, his children's governess, was a frail middle-aged spinster who was most unsuited to sea travel. The slightest motion of the ship sent her moaning to her bunk, and whilst their father flirted openly with Mrs. O'Brien (and Jane, who was not innocent of worldly ways, suspected that his intentions were not altogether honourable), the obliging Miss Terrill kept an eye on spoiled, capricious little Dolly and affectionate Rodney.

She agreed to attempt a written story, telling herself that anyone who could hold a pen could do better than Mrs.

O'Brien's coy doggerel. Having gained his point, Sandford moved away to more congenial company, and she resolutely choked down a mixture of hurt and anger.

Dorcas MacBride, concerned as she was with her own responsibilities, noticed what was happening and spoke to her niece about it.

"Don't let Mr. Sandford impose on you," she warned. "He is from Victoria, you know, and they're all the same! Forever taking advantage."

Jane had already noticed, with some astonishment, that there was a definite rift betwixt those passengers from the two separate Australian states of New South Wales and Victoria. The latter, which had until 1851 been part of the former, was considered an upstart by those from the mother colony, and for their part, the Victorians thought the Sydney-siders, as they quaintly called those from New South Wales, a stodgy lot out to undermine enterprising Victoria and its flourishing, gold-rich capital, Melbourne.

"I don't mind the children," said Jane,

in reply to her aunt's remonstrance. "Dolly can be rather difficult, but I can sympathise, having lost my own mother at an early age."

"That is not the point," rejoindered Mrs. MacBride, squinting a little as she threaded a needle. "Mr. Sandford has a governess with him, and I'm quite sure the woman is also taking advantage of your kindness."

"I'm quite sure that isn't the case. Poor Miss Lark really does seem to be in bad health."

Aunt Dorcas pursed her lips, still not convinced. She stitched for about half a minute, and then spoke again, whilst her niece re-hemmed one of Alice's dresses, which had needed letting down.

"Sandford's wife left him, you know. Oh, she is dead, but they were apart when she died. Mrs. Duncan — she is from Melbourne — told me that it was all quite a scandal. Apparently Mrs. Sandford ran away with a 'digger' while she was — hum — expecting Rodney."

Ordinarily, Aunt Dorcas would not have discussed such delicate matters with an unmarried girl, but she felt that the circumstances needed it.

"*He* was supposed to be the youngest son of an aristocratic family back Home. Jack Someone-or-another. I can't recall the exact name. His father was said to be an earl from the north of England. Still, so many of these people who come into Australia tell all sorts of stories about themselves, and I would take that with a grain of salt!"

Now Mrs. MacBride lowered her voice. She was a very proper person, and she must have debated long and hard with herself before deciding to pass on this scandal to Jane.

"She died giving birth to little Rodney. There seems to have been no doubt that it was Sandford's child. Of course, people do wonder, and the little fellow really does not resemble Mr. Sandford, but I believe the mother was slight and fair. Poor Mr. Sandford! What humiliation! He left his property in the hands of his brother-in-law, and it was believed at the time that he had settled in England for good."

She concluded the story by saying that ship's gossip had it that he was returning to Australia because of the little girl's health.

"So that is why he looks so sad!" burst out Jane.

"My dear, a woman in *that* condition does not leave a perfectly good husband without a reason."

Angry words of protest rose to Jane's lips, but in time she forced them back. Aunt Dorcas had a particular look on her face. Without putting it into words, she was reminding Jane that she was an heiress and a young woman of importance. She should not be lowering herself by acting as nursemaid for the children of a man over whose past there hung a question mark.

At the same time, she did not seem to suspect the intensity of feeling which Simon Sandford aroused in Jane.

A few nights later, there was a violent and terrifying storm, the first of several to be encountered as the *Kincardine* pressed further into the waters of the vast southern ocean wastes. The lightning flashed and the ship heaved, and poor Miss Lark quietly died. Too late, her persistent complaint was diagnosed not as *mal de mer*, but a malignancy.

"Poor soul," said Aunt Dorcas, apparently forgetting her earlier uncharitable comments. "I cannot even recall what she looked like. I doubt whether I ever saw her."

Miss Lark was buried in the grey tossing sea, and during the funeral service which was conducted by the captain, Jane found herself standing next to Sandford.

"I shouldn't have let her come," said Miss Lark's former employer, when it was all over. "She begged me. She was very fond of the children, but she must have known that she was ill."

"She was a single woman of no means," said Jane, flatly, unable to help speaking her mind. "She was no longer young, and sick. If she'd left your employ, what would have happened to her?"

Sandford looked startled at her outspokenness, but there was also in his expression a query. Out of the corner of her eye, Jane saw Mrs. O'Brien's annoyed toss of the head. Mrs. O'Brien had wept noisily all through the service, as if bereaved of a dear and valued friend. It made Jane even angrier, furious for all the decent, deprived, gently raised women for whom there was no real place in a hard and uncaring world. But for the Grace of God — helped along, one had to confess, by Papa — she could have eventually found herself in that same position.

"I've seen many like her," she continued. "Poverty comes in many forms, Mr. Sandford. We hear so much about the squalid sort, but at least, there is the advantage of not having to keep up appearances. Genteel poverty is bitterly cruel. Imagine having to pretend that one is not really hungry and that using tea leaves twice is sensible, so that one can afford a scrap of ribbon in order that one's Sunday bonnet won't betray just how straitened things are."

She turned and walked away, leaving the man speechless. Later, of course, she was sorry that she had let her tongue run away with her, for she was sure that she had spoiled what little chance she had of making a favourable impression on Simon Sandford.

The children took their governess's death in the separate ways which Jane now recognised as typical of them. Rodney, trying hard to be a little man, fought hard to keep back his tears, and then succumbed. He had liked Miss Lark. She always played a little game with him when she tucked him up of a night. His sister's eyes were strangely tearless as Jane comforted the little boy.

"Everyone dies," she said, calmly. "My mama died, and your papa died." And she turned her small back to go on playing with her doll.

4

IT grew very cold as the *Kincardine* plunged into higher latitudes. There were no more storytelling sessions on deck, and heavy outer clothing had to be worn when one ventured into the open air. As the fierce and aptly named Roaring Forties strained the very fibres of the huge sails, the *Kincardine* began attaining the extraordinary daily distances which kept so many faithful to sail. Bets were laid amidst the more sporting as to whether or not the ship could surpass her previous day's astonishing three hundred and seventy three sea miles, measured from noon to noon, whilst the more nervous had nightmares about rocks and icebergs.

The wind howled through the rigging, the drenching spray flew up over the bowsprit, the crew used ropes strung about as they moved on a deck slippery with water, and every joint and hinge of the ship's hull creaked and groaned.

Nevertheless, the *Kincardine* held steadily to her course, easterly below the width of the Indian Ocean, passing the dark and icy outcrop of Kerguelen Island, four men constantly at the wheel to obey every order issued by the expert and experienced captain.

One day, the wind abated for a while and the sun shone, allowing the hardier to come up on deck and stare about at the whole desolate vastness of these southern seas.

"The captain tells me we're about to turn northeast for Melbourne," said Sandford, joining Jane, who was watching a swooping albatross and wondering how any living thing could survive in such a region.

"Are you glad to be nearing your home, Mr. Sandford?" She kept her tone very formal, almost stilted, for he had avoided her since the day of Miss Lark's funeral. For herself, it had been a time of determined self-cure, trying to will herself out of her infatuation. Now that he was so near, resolves weakened, and her whole being yearned for a sign that at least he *liked* her.

"I expect I am," he answered, with a sigh. "But I'll miss England. It's a much more comfortable country — for those who aren't poor!"

She felt that he had added the last words as an extra, in case she spoke out again about poverty-stricken gentlewomen.

"And you," he continued, glancing down at her with a rare half-smile, "are you looking forward to seeing your new home?"

She did not know, but she was unusually attractive that day, for her cheeks were made rosy by the cold air, so that the black she wore flattered her.

"Yes," she replied, after a moment's consideration. "I am. My regret is that my poor father is not with me to enjoy my good fortune. I dare say you know why I am emigrating. There are few secrets on this ship."

He nodded.

"It has been whispered to me," he admitted. "You're joint heiress with Mrs. MacBride to old Horatio Wilson's fortune. And I believe we have something in common, Miss Terrill."

54

Her aunt still made no secret of the fact that she did not like Simon Sandford. He was, she said repeatedly, typical of those pushy, opportunistic people who had made fortunes down in Victoria since the gold rush. Hugh MacBride did not seem to share this possibly illogical dislike, and when Dorcas again admonished Jane for giving so much time to the Sandford children, he merely laughed and said:

"We'll be leaving them in Melbourne, and by the time we've reached Sydney, you'll be so glad to walk on land again that you'll not give them another thought."

This, thought Jane, proved that she had hidden her feelings for Sandford very successfully, and it was accepted that her only interest was in the children. Still, when Mr. Sandford suggested that they had something in common, her heart began racing.

"You now own Curwood."

"Yes, that is so."

"Your grandfather bought it from my late wife's family."

Oh, thought Jane. The MacBrides must have known that all along, but they took care not to mention it to me.

She was now beset by the uneasy feeling that the MacBrides were more perceptive about her emotions towards Mr. Sandford than she had thought, and more sensible than to mention it.

"What is Curwood like?"

She had certainly not put aside her early idea of attempting to run the property herself. Uncle Hugh disapproved, and although she did not argue, she was quietly determined to investigate the possibility when they reached Australia.

"A good property. You've heard of Bendigo where so much gold was found? Well, it's a few miles out of Bendigo. The land's rolling and fertile and well-watered, but more suitable for grazing stock than raising crops, although there used to be a good orchard and garden at Curwood homestead. Of course, part of it was overrun by diggers during the height of the rush back in 'fifty two, and they left a fearful mess. They turned acres of good land upside down."

"How on earth could they be allowed to do that?"

"Although my wife's parents leased the

land, Miss Terrill, it still belonged to the Crown. Gold also belongs to the Crown, which buys it from the miner. When the digger pays for his licence, he can go anywhere on Crown land. At one stage, there were about three thousand men within a mile of the homestead, all congregated in one valley. They turned over every square foot. Fortunately, the gold soon gave out, and they left."

Woman-like, she was more interested in the living quarters at Curwood.

"What is the house like?"

"I thought it comfortable. My own place was only twelve miles away." He paused, and stared, as if unseeing, across the darkening sea. The brief midwinter day was almost over, and the icy breeze made Jane eager to go below. "Funny, when I first went there back in 'forty eight, I thought it would be forever. I can remember riding up over the hill and looking down at the spot where I had my own homestead built, and thinking that I would stay there for the rest of my life."

"Are you going to be a pastorialist again, Mr. Sandford?"

He turned, and looked at her in a strange, intense fashion.

"I don't know what I'm going to do," he said, quite abruptly, as if regretting allowing her that peep into his past. "But for now, we'd best go below before we're both frozen into statues."

The *Kincardine* reached Melbourne's port of Sandridge on a clear, sunny morning, and those whose destination was the Victorian capital prepared to disembark. The arrival of the ship had been telegraphed from a point about sixty miles south, for Melbourne lay a few miles upstream on the banks of a river which discharged into a huge, landlocked bay, and every vessel approaching had to enter through a narrow break in the rugged coastline.

Because of this early information, quite a few friends and relatives awaited the new arrivals as a tug towed the big four-master to its berth alongside a pier stretching out from the low and uninteresting shore. This was Railway Pier, connected to Melbourne itself by a train service.

Jane, watching the activity on the

pier, could feel nothing but despondency. Some passengers were leaving, new ones would come aboard, either for the short trip to Sydney, or intending to take the long voyage back to Britain about the southern extremity of South America. Mr. Sandford was ready to go ashore, and it was unlikely that she would ever see him again. He had the children with him, and young Rodney, sighting his friend, ran to her.

"Miss Jenny," he cried, pulling at her skirts and looking up into her face. "You must come with us."

She felt the tears prickling behind her lids.

"I must go on to Sydney," she said, and stroked the child's fair, fine hair. "But perhaps I shall write you a letter."

"You've made quite a conquest. But come on, Roddy, you're going to see your aunt and uncle and cousins."

Dolly had already hauled herself up so that she could see over the rail on to the pier.

"There's Aunt Lucy!" she shrieked.

"You can't remember her, surely," said her father, astonished. "We've been away over two years, nearly three."

"That's Aunt Lucy! See, she's seen me and she's waving!"

"She's right, you know." Sandford held out his hand to Jane. "Thank you very much on behalf of the children, Miss Terrill. And every best wish for your future here in Australia."

"I believe we shall be here in Melbourne for a day or two," she responded. She was, of course, begging him to suggest that he should take her sightseeing, but he said nothing more, but picking up Rodney and with Dolly hurrying behind him, strode down the gangplank.

Sandford and his children were greeted by a stout, well dressed man in a tall black silk hat, and a still-pretty dark-haired woman who resembled Sandford sufficiently to be his sister. How strange. Jane had always imagined him to be such a solitary person, but here he was, surrounded by relatives, for there were several children too. Then, the strangest stray thought wafted into her mind. If five year old Dolly could recall her aunt after a separation of over two years, could she remember the circumstances surrounding her mother's death? She certainly was an odd little girl, brighter than average for her age, but with a coolness of disposition almost grotesque in a young child.

The thought vanished, to lie forgotten for a long time, while two other more current matters occupied her attention. Mrs. O'Brien was turning her egress from the *Kincardine* into a dramatic farewell scene. She went from one to another, breathily assuring them that she would remember them always, and even Jane, whom she had always treated with contempt, was included. Then, grandly, she swept down the gangplank, to be greeted by a stout, vulgar looking woman who was undoubtedly Mrs. O'Brien's female parent, and a lanky child of at least eleven who flung herself at the flashily dressed woman and cried out, "Mother!"

There were smiles of amusement and some knowing glances exchanged amongst those still on board. Mrs. O'Brien had gone out of her way to impress upon everyone that she was no more than twenty four years

61

of age. Quite obviously, unless she had wed much younger than usual, she had chopped off several years — always supposing that something quite disastrous had not occurred in her very early teens.

Mr. Sandford, still talking with his relatives, glanced about, saw the widow, and lifted his hat, which she took as an invitation to join his party. It infuriated the watching Jane.

Meanwhile, a slim, fair man, dressed well in city clothes, but wearing a broad-brimmed wide-awake style of headgear which advertised that he was in town from the bush, was standing on the other side of the pier, scanning the crowd as if searching for someone in particular. For a second or two, he looked up at the ship, and his eyes met Jane's. They were very blue, reminding her of Evan Whiteside, and very hard, and she had the oddest feeling that she had seen him somewhere before. A moment later, he began walking toward Sandford's group. Once, he stopped, as if hesitant, and the watching girl, curious about anything concerning Sandford, felt a tingle of shock down her spine. Never in her life had she seen such naked hatred on a man's face, and it was directed at Sandford.

Then he joined them, and they all began walking away, through the bustling crowd and the numerous vehicles, and were soon lost to sight.

The *Kincardine*'s stay in port to collect more passengers and unload cargo was the opportunity for those who still had to go on to Sydney to stretch their legs. Alas, the fine weather which had greeted them all too soon dispersed into the gales and savage rain storms more typical of the late Victorian winter. As well, Jane succumbed almost immediately to influenza, of which there was a mild epidemic in Melbourne.

It was not a mere case of the sniffles, nor a mere sore throat, but a violent attack which sent her to bed. Within a day, her condition was so worrying that a doctor was called. He advised her immediate removal to shore lodgings, where it would be possible to have a well-aired room with a fireplace. To travel to Sydney was out of the question,

63

quite leaving out the possibility of the infection spreading through the ship. He suggested a suite of rooms in a good city hotel, and the invalid was transported the several miles in a hansom, feeling more wretched with every jolt over the bad road. At her destination, she collapsed into bed and lost all practical interest in life for several days.

Lily, Mrs. MacBride's personal maid, a brusque and sensible woman of forty, was put in charge, and given firm instructions not to allow Miss Terrill to make the trip to Sydney until she was quite recovered. Vaguely, in between the miseries of throbbing head and aching back, bouts of fever and a tearing cough, Jane heard Aunt Dorcas and Uncle Hugh farewell her from a safe distance at the door. A week had passed after the onset of the illness before she felt well enough to contemplate getting up, and as she lay weakly in bed that cold morning, she told herself that today she would make the effort to arise and at least sit by the fire.

"Mr. Sandford's here, Miss," said Lily, coming in, and Jane sat upright, not noticing that Lily was in a state of great agitation.

How had he heard that she was here? It did not matter. The point was that he was worried enough about her to call. If she had not been so light-headed still, she would have queried the earliness of the hour.

"Tell him to wait. I shall be out directly."

This was the impetus she needed to make her take those first shaky steps. She climbed out of bed, donned her dressing-gown, thought briefly about dressing fully, and then dismissed the idea. Sense told her that an hour out of bed would exhaust her. Heavens, what a hag she looked! She had long come to terms with the fact that she was not a raving beauty, but there was normally in her face the smoothness of youth. Now she was hollow-eyed and greyish-pale.

Lily returned.

"He's there in the sitting-room," she said, and her voice was so strained that Jane turned in concern. Poor Lily must be going down with the horrid complaint.

"Could you help me put up my hair? It looks terrible."

A few moments with comb and pins helped.

Jane went out into the adjoining sitting-room. He stood by the window of the small apartment, staring out into the street. He wore, she noticed, a black frock coat over checked grey trousers, and his tall black hat sat on a small table by the door. He was no longer the traveller, but a city man on his way to his business affairs. Did he really miss his bush life? He fitted into the town scene so well.

He held a folded newspaper in his left hand, and when he swung about at her entry, he did not relinquish this.

"How kind of you to call. I'm sorry to greet you like this, but I've been quite ill. How did you know I was still in Melbourne?"

"I met Mr. MacBride in the street the day he sailed. May we sit down, Miss Terrill?"

Then she heard Lily weeping, and she knew that he had bad news to impart.

"What is it?" She sat down, already

tired and full of fear.

He did not reply, but held out the newspaper which he had folded to reveal a headline above a long column of tight print.

'KINCARDINE LOST'.
'One survivor'.

"Oh, no!" She could not weep, yet. The world about her seemed to have stopped, and as if in a distance, she heard her own voice ask Mr. Sandford to read out the report.

He did not reply, but recounted the story in his own words. The *Kincardine* had encountered bad weather off Sydney, and her master had made a fatal error of judgment. Instead of riding out the storm, he had decided to take his ship and her complement through the narrow entrance into Port Jackson, the safe and beautiful harbour upon which Sydney is located.

Sandford explained that the coastline in that region is rocky and dangerous, and the entrance a mere break in a line of forbidding cliffs. There was a good lighthouse on the South Head, but the master, in the poor visibility, mistook it for the beacon on the North Head, and an indentation in the line of cliffs for the entrance. The *Kincardine* had thrust into the rocky wall with the full force of her two thousand tons. She had sunk within minutes, and only one young sailor had survived, through the lucky chance of being carried on a wave high up on to a ledge. There he had clung for many hours, until the amount of debris being carried into the harbour had alerted people living nearby to the possibility of a shipwreck.

"There is no hope?"

"None. I came early in the hope that you had not yet seen the newspaper. I felt that you would prefer to have it told to you by — well, an acquaintance, at the very least."

"Six in one family! Oh, God, why did it happen?"

It was different from losing poor Papa. He had been failing for some time, and they had both accepted that his span was limited. His passing had been a painful loss, but she had been prepared.

She had been looking forward to seeing the MacBride family again in Sydney. Now they were all gone, Aunt Dorcas whose rather domineering manner hid a fund of good sense and kindliness, amiable Uncle Hugh, and the four children. It almost broke her heart to think of funny little Charlton who had so loved her stories, and of Alice, with her old-fashioned, surprisingly shrewd ways, who had shared a cabin with Jane for so many weeks.

They had all been snuffed out.

Mr. Sandford did not wish her to read the newspaper account, but as soon as he had left, she sent the grief-stricken Lily out to buy a copy, and the two women pored over it, crying together, and praying that for everyone the end had been swift.

At the official enquiry, a curious fact came to light. Although the *Kincardine*'s captain had sailed the Great Circle route from Britain to Australia and back again many times, he had never before had reason to call at Sydney. Normally, his ship would have ended her Australian run at Melbourne (and her Sydney-bound passengers would have gone on by coastal steamer) before commencing the homeward passage via Cape Horn. However, the *Kincardine*'s owners, plagued by the common problem of finding sufficient cargo and enough passengers to make the long haul back to Britain profitable, had decided to risk double port fees in the hope of overcoming the problem. Dead with him was the secret behind that aberration which had caused a skilful and experienced mariner to attempt a strange and tricky harbour entrance in shocking conditions.

For Jane, the pain of loss lasted a long time, and she never could recall a single one of Papa's sayings which helped in the slightest.

5

ACCOMPANIED by faithful Lily, Jane arrived, unannounced, at Curwood homestead during October. They had travelled north from Melbourne by coach, which journey gave them the opportunity of seeing evidence of the landscaping changes wrought by the goldseekers.

This land between Melbourne and the mining centre of Sandhurst was fertile, although hilly in places, and generally attractive, with blue ranges always in the distance to mark the horizon. To Jane, the astonishing blueness of the hills was an Australian surprise. Once the well-sprung, American-styled coach had passed the rearing might of Mount Macedon about forty miles from Melbourne, everywhere were signs of the frenzy which had turned sparsely populated land into the goal of thousands.

Where the 'rushes' had been brief, sheep now picked their way placidly through the great heaps of pale yellow clay and shale which were heaped about the paddocks. The banks of once pretty little watercourses had been stripped of the protective vegetation and had eroded into gutters, ruined by the activity of men frantically seeking gold's elusive gleam.

The small towns through which they passed were simply strings of buildings lining the main road for a considerable distance with only a few houses along the cross streets. One thing which all of these hamlets had in common was a plethora of public houses, ranging from structures little better than henhouses to quite substantial buildings constructed of the basaltic bluestone which was a reminder of a distant volcanic era.

The road itself was quite terrible. Surveyors were working along the way in preparation for improvements, but much of that presently in use was boggy and rutted, and so bad in places that alternative routes had been forced through the scrub to such an extent that the once narrow track was now several chains wide. Witness of small disasters were many, broken down drays, carts and so forth lying alongside the route, as well as the occasional dead horse or bullock providing succour for the large black crows which were, apparently, the most numerous form of bird life.

The weather was typical Victorian October, blowing a cold gale one moment, and fiercely sunny the next, so that the passengers alternately shivered and baked.

Lily declared that the small town where they had to spend the night was the messiest place she had ever seen. Jane agreed with her. Given that here was none of the grim blackness of coalmining, it appeared to the onlooker that winning gold was a chaotic business, with most of the end product comprising mud in various colours and consistencies (it had been raining heavily in the area), varied mounds of broken shale and quartz. Hereabouts, surface mining, the poor man's hope, had already given out, but nothing had been done to repair the damage. In every direction, the earth gave the impression of having been turned over by some cataclysm, and it was hard to credit that these endless heaps of subsoil on a pitted and gullied landscape, were all produced by ordinary humans with ordinary arms, using ordinary tools. Chinese still optimistically picked over these 'tailings', but mining in this little town was now concentrated underground, and ore being processed in two plants, the donkey engines and batteries making a frightful racket which the inhabitants seemed able to ignore.

"Curwood?"

When she asked mine host of the indifferent inn about her property, he looked extremely surprised.

"Well, it's a fair way, miss, and right off the coach road."

"I know that, but surely I can hire a vehicle of some kind?"

She sounded crisp, and in control, but she was beginning to doubt her wisdom. Everything seemed bigger and wilder and rougher than she had expected. She knew that she should have gone on to Sydney, but she could not face the scene of the *Kincardine* tragedy. She had to be busy, fill in her days energetically, and not dwell on the past. Papa had wished her to build a new life, and that was exactly what she was going to do.

There was another reason for this decision to follow her first inclination to run Curwood herself. It was acknowledged in the lonely nights, but never aloud.

She had hoped that, after his show of kindness on that morning, his feelings towards her might deepen. He did introduce her to his sister, Lucy Parker, but as far as Jane was concerned, he kept everything on a purely formal plane.

In those first days of recovering both from her illness and the news about the *Kincardine*, she learnt a lot about the Sandfords, for Lucy had an easy, outgoing nature, and enjoyed nothing more than talking about her family.

Their father, old Captain Sandford, now dead some years after their mother, had been an officer in Wellington's army. Like many of those who had served in the war against Napoleon, he had chosen after the end of hostilities to exchange his commission for a land grant in New South Wales. He had prospered, and eventually, had expanded his holdings to include land in the southern portion of the Australian continent, then known as the Port Phillip District, but later named Victoria.

When his twenty-year-old son had returned from completing his education in Britain, Captain Sandford had generously given him a well-watered, well-stocked 'run' of his own. It seemed only natural that the young Simon should marry pretty Sarah (Sally) Parker, daughter of the elder Sandford's old friend, who had pioneered Curwood.

The union between the two families did not stop there: Lucy had already married Sally's brother, Caleb Parker. Lucy, Jane soon realised, quite considered herself in the top layer of colonial society, but unlike her brother, she had not benefited from long periods abroad, and as a result, she was insular in her views, and could not believe that life could be better elsewhere. As for her husband, Caleb — now Papa had had a saying from Proverbs which summed up that Melbourne magnate. "He that maketh haste to be rich shall not be innocent."

The Parker parents had moved on to the South Island of New Zealand, out from Christchurch, where another brother, Sarah's twin, had also settled.

Lily did not care much for them, and made no secret of it. They were 'new money' as opposed to 'old money', which Jane found amusing, as no Australian fortune could be more than seventy years old, the first settlement having been established in 1788. In some mysterious way, the Wilson money was better. Grandfather Wilson had arrived before the turn of the century as a free settler, and this made him superior to those who had emigrated after Napoleon's war rather than eke out lives as half-pay officers.

About three weeks slipped by quietly. She received letters from the Sydney solicitors handling her grandfather's estate which explained that her aunt's death would not affect her own inheritance. Mrs. MacBride's share of the estate would, of course, be held in trust for the surviving children who had remained in England. The firm's Melbourne representative would assist Miss Terrill in every way possible, but it was respectfully suggested that she should move to Sydney as soon as practicable.

"We could go by coach," said Lily. She had relatives in Sydney, and wanted to go back there. At the same time, she made it clear, she felt that she owed it to Mrs. MacBride to stay with Miss Terrill. Perhaps Miss Terrill would be returning to England now that she had no kin in this country?

"No. I am not going back."

There were MacBrides in Britain, she explained, to take over the guardianship of the three orphans. There was no necessity for her to return. Lily sent her one of her knowing looks. Without uttering a sound, she implied that the reason why Miss Terrill lingered in Melbourne was that Mr. Sandford poor Mrs. MacBride had had such a down on.

At their first interview, Jane mentioned to the Melbourne solicitor handling her affairs that she had considered taking up residence at Curwood. He returned with the now familiar reasons why she should not. She knew nothing about Australian conditions, she was, ahem, a little youthful, and above all, by inference, she was female.

Then, *it* happened, and fortunately, she was alone at the time, for to have Lily sniff and toss her sandy head in that awful 'I told you so' way would have been too much to bear. Jane saw Mr. Sandford driving the odious Mrs. O'Brien about the town in a smart little phaeton. Her small, black-clad figure straightened. What a fool she was, hanging about Melbourne like a lovesick maiden in a romance! It was high time she pulled herself together! Why should she live in rented rooms when she owned a house in the country?

The solicitor, poor man, was rather flabbergasted when his formerly pale and irresolute client made her determined announcement. She was leaving tomorrow to inspect Curwood. It was hers, and it was high time she personally inspected the property.

"There's a manager in residence," the man pointed out, tactfully, "and judging by the returns, he's doing an excellent job."

What he meant was that she should sit at home, hands folded, content to fritter away her days in idleness.

"I'm sure we can come to a satisfactory agreement," she replied, tersely.

He paused before replying, drumming a forefinger lightly on the top of his desk, plainly trying to think of a way to dissuade this stubborn young lady from upsetting an applecart which ran smoothly and profitably.

"Miss Terrill. Curwood lies in the heart of the gold country. There are great numbers of — ahem — rather coarse men moving about that area."

"That is something I shall worry about when the time comes," she replied, in a clear and bell-like voice.

When the time came, some days later, at Curwood, she was much less confident.

She hired a man to drive herself and Lily the last several miles to her intended home. At first, the two women found much to divert them. The narrow dirt track wound over hills and through vales, the country being lush and green from recent spring rains. Sheep and cattle fed contentedly, in what back Home were called fields but here were paddocks, fenced crudely with posts and rails.

Herons picked gracefully about small pools, and cocktatoos screeched through the scattered clumps of fine old trees, their carefully posted look-out birds giving ample warning to the rest of the flock that strangers were approaching. An occasional laughing jackass, that brown and fawn member of the kingfisher tribe also called kookaburra, cackled madly as they passed, and Lily pointed out a hawk hovering above a scattering of huge grey rocks. Then, as mile followed jolting mile, interest faded.

"It does seem a very isolated place," ventured Jane to the taciturn person who held the reins.

"Well, it ain't close to town," he muttered through a savage black beard, and a few moments elapsed before she realised that by 'town' he meant that muddy and ramshackle hamlet they had left.

They stopped to rest the horses, and the taciturn man gathered a few twigs and bits of bark and lit a small fire, upon which he boiled up a quart pot of water — referring to it as his billycan — and brewed some extremely black and bitter tea, which he served in tin pannikins, without milk or sugar. Both Jane and her maid thought it horrible, but they were thirsty and there was nothing else offering.

The track now edged its way along a ridge overlooking a narrow valley on one side and fairly flat country on the other. For a short distance, the valley was as wild as Australian bush could be, a tangle of trees and shrubbery, but abruptly, it became a desert of eroded slopes, stripped of all vegetation, and pitted by the now familiar abandoned mine shafts. Dominating all was a most remarkable structure, spanning the width of the valley, here about a hundred yards, from a heap of great jumbled rocks on the opposite ridge to a small artificial pond. Built with some degree of engineering skill, it was constructed entirely of wood, the uprights being the straight boles of the stringbark variety of gum tree. These in turn supported the aqueduct itself, made of planks, and weathered, like the rest, into a silvery grey.

"Why was the flume built there?"

asked Jane. She had seen other edifices, less primitive, of this kind in industrial areas back Home.

"You mean the race," muttered the bearded man. "Race is what we calls it 'ereabouts. Brings water over for puddlin'."

"Double Dutch," muttered Lily, under her breath.

Jane shivered, although the sun was now shining brightly. The place had about it a desolation which filled her with a strange sense, almost premonition. In a moment, her usual matter of factness reasserted itself. Why did men have to make things so ugly? Papa had a favourite quotation for such grim scenes. "An habitation of dragons, and a court for owls."

Yet, not very much further on, was a crudely built wooden shack at the side of the track, overlooking the valley, and it was inhabited. Smoke came from the chimney, and there was a considerable amount of washing on a line. Two cows munched at poor grass, some hens scattered as the dogcart approached, and a skinny woman with several children at her skirts emerged from the shack and stared at them.

"Who lives in such a place?"

"That's the Wellses," said the driver, and he waved at Mrs. Wells, who raised a hand back.

"But isn't that Curwood land?" Jane had now identified the valley as the one described to her by Simon Sandford, the site of a brief but populous 'rush'.

"In a manner o' speakin', yes, but Joe Wells has got 'is mining rights. Long as he keeps minin' he can live there."

"But they look so poor! And where do the children go to school?"

Jane was no stranger to the poverty of England's back streets. During their leaner periods, she and Papa had lodged in some very humble abodes, and to her experienced eye, Mrs. Wells and family looked very little better off than the poorest back Home.

"There ain't no schools round 'ere. No call for it."

"But why on earth do they stay there?"

"Joe Wells's got a shaft back there. Can't see it from the track. They get by." Now that the taciturn man had a subject he could get his teeth into, he was becoming voluble. "When the government — the government what we elected — does the right thing by those what elected it, and sells off Crown land free and open, with no dealin's behind closed doors, people like the Wellses'll be able to settle, decent like, on farms."

Lily went bright red with indignation, but Jane nudged her quickly. Whatever the rights and wrongs of the land question, this was no place to argue about it. During talks with the solicitor in Melbourne, Jane had been told that a large sum of money had been set aside in a special fund for the purpose of buying up leased land when it became available. At the time, unaware that there were many who had bitter feelings on the subject, she had thought it an excellent idea.

For now, she and Lily were at the mercy of their driver. If he decided to tip them out and leave them, they would have to find their way to Curwood as best they could.

Yet, she need not have worried, for they were now within shouting distance of the homestead, set a little apart from its attendant cluster of outbuildings and all the usual appurtenances of a working sheep run. No wonder the Parkers had sold out to her grandfather! With three thousand diggers almost on their doorstep, life must have become very trying.

At first, Curwood homestead was prepossessing. It was a solidly built two storeyed house of stone, set in a fenced garden of large proportions, with an orchard to the rear. As she was helped down from the cart outside the picket gate, Jane felt a pleasurable beating of the heart. It *was* worth the coming. In all her life, she had never had a permanent home, and whatever griefs and disappointments lay behind, everything in the future was going to be better.

However, as she stepped into the garden, she realised that the first good impression was illusory. Without doubt, this had once been a nicely laid out, carefully tended garden, most of the plants being of a kind popular in Australia as not requiring much water during the hot, dry summer. There were aloes, geraniums, daisy bushes of different kinds, a rambling rose which had not been pruned for a long time, two or three varieties of succulents which had grown shapeless and distorted, and what looked like a choked out clump of jonquils. Anything gentler had disappeared under tall grass, which in turn was fighting through the dead remains of several crops of its own species.

There was a verandah with a slightly raised flagged floor along the front and sides of the house, and this was littered with dead leaves and an assortment of bottles, old boots and broken garden tools.

"What a mess!" snapped Lily. "They must live like pigs!"

Just then, the two women heard a hiss and a flapping, and saw coming straight towards them a very large and indignant gander. This was no time for niceties. The front door was propped open with a rock, and they both dashed inside, Lily kicking aside the rock, and slammed the door behind themselves.

"Is anyone at home?" called out Jane, nervously, whilst the infuriated gander pecked at the outside of the door.

There was no answer. The house seemed deserted, and had that stuffy, unpleasant smell of a dwelling which is not cleaned as often as it should be.

"Filthy!" snorted Lily. "And look in there!"

There was what should have been a drawing-room, a finely proportioned, high-ceilinged room with tall windows opening on to the side garden. The glass was grimy, and the curtains faded and filthy. Yet, this was obviously a much-used room. There was a camp bed, unmade, at one side, there were ashes in the fireplace, a couple of empty bottles on the floor, two reasonably good chairs, a table with its feet standing in old meat tins (to discourage ants) and a litter of cigar butts. There was also a heap of old clothing in one corner which appeared to be used as a bed by a large dog.

"Who the hell are you?"

The voice was loud, crude, and hostile, and matched its owner, a short, solid man with a red face showing above one of those fierce beards which were the hallmark of the Australian bush dweller. He held a short handled whip in one hand, and a sweat-stained felt hat in the other. Behind him was the large dog which the two newcomers had deduced shared the room. It was a rangy crossbred beast, probably part greyhound but with something fairly heavy in its ancestry, making it suitable for hunting kangaroos.

"And may I ask the same of you?"

If you are in the right, dear Papa always said, act like it, although it was rather hard with that huge dog baring its teeth and slavering. Her small but straight stance appeared to take the bearded man aback.

"You're trespassing," he said, after a moment. "I reckon you've come to the wrong place. I'll give Billy Harden a call and set you on your way."

Billy Harden was the man who had driven them hither.

"But this is Curwood? I am the new owner."

"This is Curwood, orright, and I'm the manager. Now, miss, I ain't had no information about anyone movin' in. From what I've had in letters, things are to go on as before."

The large dog suddenly lost interest, and collapsed on to its bed, where it rested its nose on its paws and made funny little noises. What a relief, thought Jane, preparing herself for the next round.

"I am Jane Terrill, the late Mrs. MacBride's niece. I inherited Curwood from Mr. Horatio Wilson, my grand-father, and I intend to live here. I would like to be shown around, and have some preparations made for my own accommodation and that of my maid."

A pair of black eyes in the red face narrowed, and the thin mouth, half hidden under the beard, tightened.

"Well, I'm telling you right now, Miss What's-yer-name, I ain't working for no woman."

She could scarcely believe her ears.

At the same time, outside, Billy Harden had decided to bring in the luggage, and was now shielding himself against the aggressive gander with Jane's portmanteau.

"'Scuse me," said the manager, and pushing open a window, he yelled at the large bird in language which made Lily cover her ears. Strangely enough, the bird seemed to understand, and retreated.

"Now, miss," continued the manager, turning back, "as you see, I live in the house. If you're planning to stay, I don't know where. There's only the men's living quarters a bit away. The manager's cottage was burnt down Christmas twelve month."

He spoke as if the matter were now settled. Billy Harden placed her portmanteau and Lily's carpet bag on the floor, and stood indeterminately, as if turning over in his mind whether to pick them up and take them out again.

"You may bring in my trunk," said Jane.

The manager tried a new tactic.

"How do I know you're the owner?" he asked, head cocked on one side.

"I've a letter from the Melbourne solicitor handling my part of the Wilson estate."

"It's what I said," he retorted. "I ain't ever worked for a woman, and I ain't starting now. If you think you can run Curwood, you're welcome to try. But I'm goin' soon's I pack me things."

Billy Harden brought in the small trunk, and waited nervously until she took some notice of him.

"I'm goin' now, Miss Terrill, if you're not comin' back," he whispered, whilst the manager stumped outside, slapping the whip handle against his thigh and yelling at the dog to follow him, which it did after a few melancholy whimpers.

"What on earth is wrong with that man?" Jane demanded.

When things are going wrong, Papa had always said, one must act with determination. Actually, she wanted to cry on the nearest sympathetic shoulder, but here she was, at Curwood, which was far from being the haven she had anticipated, and she had to make the best of things.

"Mr. Wheeler don't like women, Miss Terrill. He's a good manager, though."

"Quite obviously, I shall need a new manager."

"I'll be off, if you don't mind."

How scared he sounded, as if he

were afraid of being accused of having betrayed the difficult Mr. Wheeler.

"No, wait. I shall write a letter immediately, and you shall post it for me. And Lily, do look about the house, so that I can order what we need to carry on for the time being."

"There's stores here, miss. They buy everything in bulk every six months."

"Sheets? Clean crockery? I shall expect you to place an order at the store back in the town and bring the items *tomorrow*."

The solicitor in Melbourne had been right, of course. She should have left things at Curwood exactly as they were.

6

SHE had a dream, a terrible dream. Like all nightmares, it was nonsense, but very real while she was experiencing it.

Jane took a long time to go to sleep that first night at Curwood. Lily, displaying an unexpected nervousness, had suggested that they sleep in the same room, but Jane, as much as she liked and appreciated the older woman, felt that things must start as they were to continue. Therefore, she claimed the largest upstairs bedroom for her own, and settled uneasily on a palliasse laid straight on to the bare floorboards.

She was overtired, and upset, and conscious that she had undertaken something she was not capable of handling. The makeshift bed was uncomfortable, and the night full of little sounds, some of which she could identify and others which were puzzling. Sheep making noises in the distance, a dog barking, a horse whinnying restlessly in the stables, a shout from the men's quarters — these were irritating but safe. As well, there were odd little thumps, eerie sounds which she hoped were uttered by night birds, and scratchings and rustlings which had her up and looking out of the window, straining her eyes against the darkness, a dozen times.

On the last occasion, the moon had risen, and the tangled ruin of a garden was starkly black and white, and beyond it, etched in outline, was the flume near the Wells' shack. Funny, she had not been aware earlier that it was visible from the upstairs windows of the house.

There was an owl, too, on the picket gate, which was swinging on its hinges. It was a very large owl, and it hooted ominously, which was strange, because standing within three feet of it was a man wearing a wide-brimmed hat. He then walked slowly towards the front door, and although she was above, she could see him quite clearly, as if she were facing him. It was the slim man with hard blue eyes she had seen on that day at Railway Pier.

He was staring at her, with that expression of hatred she recalled, and she knew that she had to run away, but she could not. The rambling rose had caught her skirt, and she was helpless, while he reached out towards her.

"Jenny, Jenny," he said, and it was Evan Whiteside's voice, and then he was no longer the slim man, but solid Whiteside, sneering, a powerful hand grabbing her left wrist. "You thought you could hide, didn't you? But you can never hide, Jenny!"

Jane awoke at that instant, shaking and yet relieved, but half believing that the events had actually taken place. As she calmed, she rationalised the dream. Of course, when she had seen the stripped valley, she had thought of the biblical description, what was it? An habitation of dragons, and a court for owls. But nonetheless, illogically perhaps, she was shaken. There was no reason on earth why Whiteside should follow her to Australia: it simply would not be worth his while.

As for the slim man with the hard

blue eyes, so much had happened since that brief glimpse on the pier that she had not given him another thought, and neither Lucy Parker nor her brother Simon Sandford had mentioned him.

What would she do if Evan Whiteside did find her? She told herself resolutely that she must not waste time thinking about things unlikely to happen. Likewise, it was stupid to think about the past. She had to grapple with the difficult present. If she kept her head, and stood firm, affairs would straighten themselves. As Papa so often said, 'Better is the end of a thing than the beginning thereof.'

Just as resolutely, she would not think about Simon Sandford. There was to be no more daydreaming, and certainly no more weeping into her pillow.

During the following days, it became increasingly difficult to remain optimistic. The manager carried out his threat and left. What was worse than losing that bullying misogynist, Mr. Wheeler, was that two of his faithful followers went at the same time. They were, respectively, the blacksmith and the cook, and they asked that their outstanding wages be sent on to an inn in one of the little towns along the Melbourne road.

"They'll drink it up in an hour," sniffed Lily.

Jane's own first response was "Good riddance!" but she soon found out that those two men were probably the most essential persons on a big grazing property. The blacksmith not only made horseshoes, but handled every repair involving metal, as well as producing nails and various specialised tools as required. She managed to coax one of the other men into taking the job of cook, but this only partly solved the problem.

Every employee at Curwood was virtually a specialist. Some looked after the needs of the animals, some spent most of their time moving supplies to the outlying huts which provided primitive living quarters for the shepherds, and some were simply labourers. No one, it appeared, could tell her how much flour or sugar was needed in a week, or how much she should pay casual workers.

"They don't want to," grumbled Lily, who made no bones about being sick to death of the whole venture.

"I should receive an answer to my letter any day now," said Jane, keeping her fingers crossed that she had done the wise thing in writing to Caleb Parker rather than to the solicitor, who would, she felt sure, say 'I told you so.'

As if the whole situation were not miserable enough, rain set in and poured down relentlessly. Lily was openly mutinous, and had been for two days. She was off back to Melbourne, and then on the packet to Sydney, she said. There was plenty of ladies' maid work about for a good woman, and not slaves' work, either, with a blunt reference to the heavy cleaning and the cooking which had been her lot since coming to Curwood. She was not going to stay in this house with practically no furniture and all those men, not much better than savages, some of them, prowling about outside. She was sorry, Miss Terrill, but there it was. She felt under an obligation because of the way she had promised poor Mrs. MacBride, God rest her soul, to keep an eye on Miss Terrill, but Mrs. MacBride would not have expected her to go out into the wilds. The MacBride property, out of Sydney, now that was a showplace, a pleasure to stay at, and there was always the Sydney house near the water in the hot summer months.

"I'll own," said Jane, through gritted teeth, "that I should have been more cautious, but as soon as someone arrives to take charge, I shall return to Melbourne, but only to purchase suitable furniture and whatever else I need. This is my home, Lily, and whether or not you stay is your decision."

At this point in the discussion, Lily let out a piercing scream. The two women were occupying themselves by hemming sheets cut from the enormous length of material brought by Billy Harden the previous week. They were seated in the large room which had been Wheeler's living quarters, and although it was now much cleaner, it was almost bare except for the old table, much scrubbed, and the chairs. To counteract the depressing damp, a fire blazed in the chimney place, but they now learnt that more than firewood had been carried indoors. Something long and thin and black and unmistakably serpentine emerged from the stacked logs and sped under the table, where it paused, as if considering its next move.

Lily jumped up on to a chair, still screaming, far removed from her usual dour, practical self, and quite forgetting modesty, she hitched up her skirts a good ten inches.

At this very instant, there was a knock on the front door. It seemed like a miracle to Jane, who had been debating whether to grab the poker and try to kill the snake herself, or whether to bolt outside in the hope of finding one of the men.

She ran out through the unfurnished entrance hall, and flung open the door, forgetting her fear in one supreme moment of joyous astonishment.

"Mr. Sandford!"

He stepped inside, divesting himself of the oilskins he wore over his riding clothes.

"What on earth's happening?" he demanded, striding into the drawing-room, and then assessing the situation at a glance.

"Well," he said, picking up the poker,

"I can't get at him while he's under the table. Miss Terrill, be brave, go to the far end, and see if you can move the table back towards the far wall."

Lily, as astonished as Jane at the man's arrival, and impressed by his manner, stopped screaming and watched in staring-eyed fascination. Jane took a deep breath, crept to the spot indicated, and pulled the table back a few inches. The rasping on the bare boards had the desired effect. The snake slithered with amazing speed back towards the firewood, and Sandford struck, with sure aim, at a spot behind its small, flat head, breaking its spine. It twitched convulsively across the floor, but he assured them both, after a few moments, that it was quite dead, and to prove his point, picked it up by the tail and hurried outside with the body.

Jane supported herself against the table, overcome briefly by faintness. Lily dismounted from the chair, recovering quickly from her fright, and her expression was now dubious.

"And what is Mr. Sandford doing here?" she asked, her tone hinting at all sorts of immorality.

"I don't know," whispered Jane. "I'm as much in the dark as you are." She knew that her faintness was almost as much due to the surprise of his arrival as to the episode of the snake. There was also the thought, barely permitted, that he had heard from Caleb Parker of her predicament and had hastened to help her. "Please be so good as to make us some tea."

"I'll have to make it here. I let the kitchen fire die down."

"All right. Bring the kettle and whatever we need. But, Lily, let me talk to Mr. Sandford alone for a little."

As soon as Lily had gone, she sank wearily into a chair, and Sandford, returning from his mission, instantly expressed his concern.

"Oh, Mr. Sandford, everything that could has gone wrong. I daresay Mr. Parker told you about my letter."

"My brother-in-law and I are not close," he said, gravely. "You will have to explain."

She quickly told him about Wheeler, and the blacksmith, and not knowing what to do. "And even that sheeting!

The storekeeper sent me at least five times as much as we need. He must think I am opening a hospital."

"I can put your mind to rest on one score, at least. I met your cook and the blacksmith at Kilmore on the way up from Melbourne. They were both very sorry for themselves and asked me whether I knew of anything offering. I know them, you see, from the old days. They're a pair of 'old hands' as you probably know, and had been with the Parkers for many years."

She had been told by one of the other men that the recalcitrant pair had been transported.

"With so many men giving up gold mining, it's hard for anyone to find work, let alone a man with a record. I advised them to come back on the chance that you hadn't replaced them, and I said I'd put in a good word for them. They'll be here tomorrow or the next day — they're walking, of course."

"Oh, thank you. I don't know where to start enquiring, to be truthful." Then, rather shyly: "Were you passing by, Mr. Sandford?"

"No, I came to see you."

This, she did not expect, and she felt hot colour spread across her cheeks, for hoping and dreaming were, she knew, far apart from reality. He was very serious, with that intent, brooding look which always made her weak and vulnerable.

Fortunately, Lily bustled in with the tea things, which she set down on the table with a clatter before attending to the kettle, which by now was steaming furiously. Mr. Wheeler had used the drawing-room fireplace for minor cooking, and had installed an iron stand with a freeswinging arm from which to hang either pot or kettle, and sometimes, judging by the mess in the fireplace which had taken so long to clear up, an occasional piece of meat.

"I wished to know whether you would consider selling Curwood to me."

What a good thing that Lily had come in just at that instant! Jane realised that she had put quite the wrong interpretation on his words. What an idiotic, romantic fool she was. She poured tea before replying.

"No, Mr. Sandford, I should not

consider selling. This is my inheritance, and I feel sure that once I have overcome certain problems, I shall manage very well indeed."

He drank his very hot tea with every sign of satisfaction.

"Ah," he said, "that was an excellent brew."

If he hoped to flatter Lily, he failed, for she left the room as he spoke.

"Now, Miss Terrill," he went on, "you must tell me something. Why did you bolt?"

"Bolt?" She sounded cool, even a little amused. "I came here to inspect my property. It seemed wise to make the journey before the heat of summer. It was always my intention to take up residence here. I think we discussed it on board ship."

"You should have said goodbye to us all." He felt in a pocket. "The children gave me a letter for you."

He handed her a folded rectangle of paper, and when she opened it out, she found herself laughing, and yet there was a choke in her throat. Dolly had painstakingly drawn a misshapen creature and spelled out the word 'cat', and there was a scrawl underneath which was presumably Roddy's attempt at writing his name.

"Are they well? I do think of them often . . . and of my poor little cousins."

They were both silent for some moments.

"I'll write them a short note before you leave, Mr. Sandford. I'm sorry you came so far for nothing."

"Oh, I've another place in mind. Curwood was my first choice, but to be honest, I think I knew that it was a forlorn hope."

The sun had come out, as it does often at the end of a very wet day, and Sandford suggested, after requesting that he might stay the night in the men's quarters, that they take a turn about the garden before dark. As they walked, she told him about the gander, now banished to a pen a safe distance from the house, and he laughed, but added the rider that she should find herself a good watchdog.

He went on to say that he was shocked at the way in which the garden had been allowed to go to rack and ruin. The trees in the orchard had obviously not been pruned in years, and that long grass and other rubbish was not only a harbour for snakes, but a fire hazard with the hot summer not far ahead.

They reached a spot where, looking up, she saw the setting suns rays reflected upon the window of the room in which she slept, and she shuddered, involuntarily.

"Now, what's wrong, Miss Terrill? Did that gander walk over your grave?"

"No, I remembered something. A nightmare I had on the first night I was here. It was quite silly, but horrible."

"From all accounts, Miss Terrill, your arrival here was a nightmare!"

She would have liked very much to ask him about the slim man with blue eyes she had seen from her vantage point on the *Kincardine*, for revived in her mind was the absolute hatred with which the unknown had regarded Sandford. Jane was unashamedly in love with the man at her side, and desperately, she wished to protect him. Papa had instilled in her

108

the necessity of keeping a still tongue when proper.

'As a jewel of gold in a swine's snout, so is a fair woman which is without discretion,' he had said.

Perhaps she was not fair and beautiful, but she was a woman, and she did not wish Mr. Sandford to consider her forward, or worse still, eccentric.

So, she shifted the conversation away from nightmares, and asked his advice about the fruit trees. He told her that he was not an expert in horticulture, but it was definitely too late to prune them this year, but perhaps she could instruct someone to cut away the dead wood and remove the weeds from the ground. He was sure, too, that in former times there had been small channels betwixt the rows with which to irrigate the orchard in summer. There was a spring at the upper end of the orchard which had always provided good water which not only nourished the fruit trees, but also grew excellent pumpkins and watermelons.

She hung upon every word of his advice, depending upon him more with every passing moment, and felt nothing but misery because he would be leaving so soon.

The next morning, she expected him to be gone at first light, but he delighted her, when she went out to make her farewells, by saying that his horse seemed to have gone lame. He did recall that the poor beast had slipped in the mud a hundred or so yards from the homestead, and must have strained a fetlock. Nothing serious, but Bevis needed a day's rest.

Lily made her own feelings clear when Jane asked whether it would be possible to put together a picnic luncheon. Mr. Sandford, whilst apologising for imposing further on Miss Terrill's hospitality, had suggested harnessing up the little cart he had noticed out in the stables, and going for a drive about the Curwood land. Jane had no idea how the sparkle in her eyes betrayed her as she accepted this offer.

Still, remembering her dignity, she tried to sound practical as she reminded Lily that she could not ride a horse, nor yet handle a vehicle herself, but Lily pursed her lips and muttered that there was little in the house suitable for a picnic basket.

"He's making himself at home," grumbled the servant as she poked about in the larder.

"Oh, Lily. He's a friend. His sister was very kind to me during our stay in Melbourne. Aunt Dorcas was a dear, good woman, but you mustn't allow yourself to be influenced by her likes and dislikes for the rest of your life."

As she spoke, a remembrance of the hated Mrs. O'Brien came into her mind, but she resolutely dismissed the recollection.

"She was a good judge of character, Miss Jane."

There was something proprietary in that 'Miss Jane', as if Lily did not relish the idea of their relationship changing. Her expression, too, was hard and rather angry.

"I don't recall her ever being wrong," she continued, slicing cold meat as if performing an execution. "She didn't like Mr. Sandford, and she didn't like that common piece, Mrs. O'Brien, neither. You must own he's a man of funny tastes, going after *her*!"

This almost uncanny picking up of her

own thoughts angered Jane.

"Lily, I've been here for more than a fortnight, and I've seen nothing past the woolshed beyond what we passed on our way from Melbourne. I would like to inspect my own property. Mr. Sandford is knowledgeable about such things, and I need all the advice he can give me. So, I do not wish to hear any more of your silly gossip."

As if to match her own joyful anticipation, the day, dull early, soon cleared away into brilliant sunshine. His memory, Simon Sandford confessed as he took up the reins, was a little vague as to the tracks about Curwood, and no doubt much had changed, but he would do his best.

For a moment, there was a cloud across the happiness of having him to herself. The old days at Curwood, for him, were the days when his late wife, pretty faithless Sarah, had been the daughter of the house here. Yet, apparently, time had softened his memories, for he no longer seemed the sad, brooding man who had rescued her from Evan Whiteside in Bristol.

As they progressed along a faintly

marked track, pausing now and then to allow sheep to move from their path, he discussed the state of affairs at Curwood. The place was obviously sound, he said, but from what he could see, Mr. Wheeler had concentrated on pleasing his superiors with high profits at the cost of letting things run down. He hoped that Miss Terrill realised that the big returns could not continue if she lived here permanently. She would have to employ more household help, including at least one gardener, and do something about restocking the stables. Then the manager's house would have to be rebuilt for a family man, for to employ a bachelor manager would invite scandalous talk.

"I'm quite aware of all that," she returned, frostily. Her life with her father had taught her to be perhaps a little more independent than the usual run of young lady, and although she was in love, she still resented the sort of male superiority which assumed that she was unable to grasp the obvious. "As I told you yesterday, I've written to Mr. Parker requesting his help in finding a manager,

113

and I'm sure that I'm quite capable of making a proper decision."

"It's strange Caleb didn't mention it to me," he mused. "Still, as I said, we aren't close."

"I am hoping for a reply very shortly."

"You should have written to me," he reproached her. "Caleb is a city man through and through."

Jane did not know how to reply, but fortunately, he did not pursue the subject, but suggested that they take a divergent track which, if his memory served him right, led to the highest point on the Curwood property. The elderly horse, the best offering since Wheeler had taken his own smart mount away with him, ambled up the incline without enthusiasm, pausing once or twice as if protesting that it was really too much. For the first quarter of a mile, they were in amidst one of the few extensive stands of tall timber left on the run, and she did not rightly realise where they were. By this time, the sun was directly overhead, and when he suggested that they stop at a small clearing to eat, she was more than agreeable.

In spite of Lily's forebodings, Sandford's behaviour could not have been more correct, and after a while, he even voiced a doubt whether they should have brought her servant with them for the sake of propriety.

"She has duties at the house," said Jane, throwing a small piece of bread towards a yellow-breasted robin which hopped about the bark littered ground only a few feet from the seated duo. She smiled, as much at the bird as at the thought of Lily. "Oh well, she did disapprove, if you must know."

"H'm. She is something of a dragon. By the way, what is her full name?"

"Lily Fields."

He laughed, heartily, in a manner which seemed quite foreign to the man she had first known.

"You're joking, Miss Terrill," he accused, recovering himself.

"No. That is her name."

"It does seem strange that such a dragon should have a comic name." Then he became very grave. "I called on you, you know, several times during your illness, but she always turned me

115

away. Did she tell you?"

It was a shock. Previously, Jane had appreciated Lily's loyalty, but now the servant was becoming an enemy.

"No," she said, quietly, resolving to have things out with Lily later.

"Well, perhaps . . . No doubt, she had her reasons. You were very ill."

He began tidying away, dousing the fire upon which the inevitable billycan had been boiled, and as she packed the small amount of crockery and cutlery into the basket, he removed the hobbles from the horse.

A few minutes later they were again in open country, high on the ridge beyond that valley which had been devastated by the gold diggers. The wooden structure of the flume was ahead, appearing more rickety and weathered from this side than from the tram along which she had travelled for that first arrival at Curwood. As before, the place depressed her. The scarred, overturned soil, the pits, the falls of shale from the slopes, and the pathetic shack owned by the Wells family all filled her with a sense of melancholy. As if to complement the dreariness of the scene, a pair of crows interrupted in their meal off the corpse of some small creature, flapped upwards, uttering their ugly caws in protest.

"You should get rid of them," he said, suddenly.

"The crows?" She had been so lost in her fancies that she did not understand at first what he meant.

"The people in that shack on the other side of the valley. Your side of the valley. There's no gold worth mentioning here now. They're using their Miner's Right to live on Curwood land and use up Curwood water. There's talk of new land laws, Miss Terrill. By the mere fact of their being there, they could claim three hundred good acres on the homestead side of the valley and pay it off under special terms to the government. Remember that most of what you think of as Curwood land is merely leased from the Crown. With the water going across in the flume, they could be very well situated. We'll leave the poor old horse here and walk the rest of the way."

She could see that the track now

inclined upwards so sharply that there was nothing for it but to follow his suggestion. The sun had become very hot, the air very still, and as they walked, the view extended in all directions. She could see the Curwood homestead from here, standing plain and square amidst its scattering of outbuildings, on the slope near the river which had attracted Captain Parker to settle there.

"That wooden aqueduct," said Sandford, returning to the subject which aggravated him, "should be knocked down, or burnt, and the water allowed to flow naturally. It would soon find its way into the river, as it did in times past. Water's always precious in this country, Miss Terrill, even when the seasons are good, like this one has been. Come along here."

He reached out, and took her hand to help her up the last steep stretch, so that they stood together on a tiny plateau with great boulders rearing behind and above them. A few feet below, Jane saw the spring which flowed down into the artificial channel supported by the framework of the flume. From this vantage point, she could pick out clearly the tunnel of the Wells mine, and the neat rows of vegetables on the lower side of the shack, invisible from the road which led directly to Curwood.

"As you can see," pointed out Sandford, "they've made themselves very comfortable by using your water. While Wells makes a pretence of mining, they're able to stay on there, on land which is properly part of your leasehold."

"Perhaps they've nowhere else to go." Sympathy for the underdog came naturally to her. She and Papa had seen, and tasted, poverty, and now that she was so well placed, she was not prepared to forget. At the same time, she saw sense in her companion's more hardheaded approach. It was one thing to be charitable, another to allow oneself to be the victim of imposition. Inexperienced though she was in rural matters, she could guess that if the waters from the spring were allowed to make their natural way down into the valley, the barren, upturned land below would soon be restored to some degree.

"Do you think that you could climb

119

up there?" he asked, not answering her last remark.

She glanced upwards, obediently, and was taken aback. He was pointing at the largest of the huge boulders, which was quite flat on top.

"It isn't as difficult as it looks," he added, taking her by the arm and leading her forward. "See?"

They were peering up through a sort of chimney in the middle of this conglomeration of rocks, and a series of ledges proved that he was right. Even in her full skirts, a young, agile person such as Jane would have little difficulty. He went first, pausing to turn back and assist her several times, so that very soon they were standing side by side on top. There was a breeze up here, and she realised that this spot would be extremely dangerous if the wind arose. She was a little breathless, as much from the excitement of feeling her hand held by his as from the effort of the climb.

The view was as surprising as it was spectacular. To the southwest spread Curwood run and beyond, rolling country of rich pastures and wooded valleys, showing the glint of watercourses still full after the rains, and blue ranges everywhere in the distance. The vista was undoubtedly Australian, with its inevitable gum trees and attendant vegetation, and a white cloud of cockatoos beyond the stark valley below. However, there was about it a placid quality reassuring to European eyes. To turn and look northwards was to be confronted with a scene so utterly at variance that Jane knew that this ridge marked a demarcation line between the Australia Felix of the early explorers and the vast and frightening inland.

There were no pastures and big, comfortable old trees. A flat featureless landscape stretched to the horizon and beyond, into a distance as vast as that of the ocean. The covering was low and scrubby, though dense, even to the bottom of the ridge, where the earth was scanty of soil and covered with broken rock and shale.

"That's what they call the Whipstick," he replied in answer to her question. He quickly added the explanation that the peculiar name had come about because timber from certain of the stunted trees was suitable for whip handles.

"Does anyone live there?"

"People won't live there until all the better country is taken up," he said. "Oh, cattle are run there, and the shooters go in after kangaroos or birds for stuffing. But it's a dangerous place. There are no landmarks, and once you're out in the scrub, it's very easy to become lost. There have been several tragedies out there, Miss Terrill, shepherds or miners who've lost their way and died of thirst and starvation. Yet, as I remember it, in early spring it was beautiful, with its wild flowers and golden wattle trees, mile after mile of them."

"I wonder how far my own land extends out into the Whipstick," she pondered.

"Not at all. This is your boundary. Captain Parker had more sense than to risk lives and stock out in that wilderness. He was here first, so he could choose."

His statement reminded Jane that Captain Parker had been Sandford's father-in-law, and she wondered whether the young couple had come up here during their courting days. A ghost, fair and pretty, and very, very young, stood at Jane's side, reminding her harshly of her own nondescript looks.

"We'd best go down. Your guardian dragon must be counting the minutes till we return," he said, teasingly. "I'll go first."

He clambered down easily, reaching upwards this time to assist her, and again she felt the excitement of physical contact as their hands locked. At the last ledge, she hesitated before jumping down, and he laughed, and held up his arms. She slid down into his embrace, and he kept his fingers intertwined behind her back.

Then he kissed her, and she yielded without thought of maidenly protest. She loved him with every shred of her being, and to feel his lips pressing harshly upon her own carried her into a state of hitherto undreamed of ecstasy.

7

HOW very hot it was!
Back Home in England, one had read of Australia's searing summers, and Aunt Dorcas had insisted on preparing for them with a trunk full of flimsy, pretty dresses, all of which had gone down with the *Kincardine*. Still, the simpler cottons which had been stitched up by a dressmaker in the nearest large town, goldmining Bendigo which now preferred to call itself Sandhurst, were probably much more suitable for a country existence.

After all, who needed frills and flounces to embellish one's looks when one had never looked better, with the bloom of early married bliss upon a face which, even to its critical owner, no longer seemed so plain. Papa had been right. Beauty did come from within, and in Jane's case, it had needed the fulfilment of a love which for long had seemed hopeless.

Who would have expected that such a dreadful and tragic year could have ended so well? Their first month together at Curwood was of such happiness that she could scarce believe it to be other than a dream. Of course, there had been Lily's sour glances to endure, but now Lily, like it or not, was banished from her former privileged position to the servants' quarters with the others who had been hired to help with the chores about the house. Lily muttered about leaving, and Jane offered her a character, but Aunt Dorcas's maid was not so easily budged. Jane guessed that for Lily it was a case of not jumping from the frying pan into the fire. Simon told her repeatedly that she was too kindhearted: she should simply tell the woman to go.

It was that same kindheartedness, over which he chided her, but respected, which permitted the Wells family to remain on their precariously held plot.

The children remained for the time being with their Aunt Lucy in Melbourne. There was still much to be done to set the interior of the homestead at Curwood in order, and as Lucy and Caleb Parker had a house at the seaside which they used during the summer months, their offer to keep the children until the newlyweds settled in was eagerly accepted.

Then, the past reached out, turning from a matter of fancies, the imagined rustle on the stairs, the aimless wondering what *she* had really been like in her foolishness and ultimate disgrace.

On a day when the heat shimmered over the paddocks, Jane and her husband of a few weeks were seated at their midday meal. Sandford was telling her that he had heard that a neighbouring 'run' was up for sale, and that it could well be the property for which he had been searching. Halfway through a sentence, he happened to glance out through the window.

"Good heavens! Am I seeing things?" he demanded, and immediately jumped up to hurry outside.

Jane had earlier noticed a small cloud of dust moving towards the homestead, but she had thought it was one of the hands returning from an errand. Now she could see that the cloud of dust had materialised into a man on horseback, and when he had dismounted and come

126

in through the gate, she was surprised that her husband should be in such haste to welcome the newcomer.

He was, at first glance, one of those 'characters' who roamed the Australian bush, eccentrics who had been unable to fit into any mould in more civilised communities. But, unlike most of those wanderers, who usually travelled on foot, this man had been well mounted, and indeed, had the touch of a crack cavalry regiment about him in spite of his peculiar and shabby garb.

A short, elderly jacket flapped open over a faded striped shirt, which in turn was tucked into the top of sagging checked trousers which had been worn long and well. The riding boots, however, were highly polished and impeccable, and were in complete contrast to the hat, which looked as if it had fallen into a muddy pool, had been dried out over a smoking fire, and then jumped on with both feet.

A ferocious full beard covering the bottom half of the visitor's face added to his general air of disreputability.

Yet, when Simon brought in the

stranger and introduced him as an old acquaintance, Robert O'Hara Burke, Inspector of Police, Jane was agreeably impressed by the well-educated and charming fashion in which this amazing Irishman spoke, and she experienced real regret when he left a couple of hours later. This man, for all his slipshod appearance when in mufti, was of a superior and well-organised intellect, and without argument, a gentleman in every sense of the word. He was, he had explained, taking a short leave of absence from his duties, and on his way to Melbourne to discuss certain confidential matters with a committee of important businessmen.

He did not reveal details, but for this extraordinary man, who had gained his spurs in the Austrian cavalry, and had left Victoria a few years previously to enlist in the Crimean conflict only to arrive too late, that discussion would lead to his tragic and lingering death. He would gain a place amidst the immortals of exploration, but at the same time remain a figure of controversy to succeeding generations.

However, Robert O'Hara Burke's brief call at Curwood, ostensibly to offer felicitations, had more immediate and worrying implications.

It had been to Jane a matter of joy and wonderment that Simon had lost his solemn and brooding look. He laughed so often these days, and if Curwood reminded him of an unhappy past, there was certainly no sign of it on the surface. Yet, from the moment they both watched Inspector Burke ride away into the heat haze, she knew that something had occurred to upset her husband.

The sombre and tragic air she had so often observed during their voyage to Australia returned. He had work to do, but when he left her, there was a mere peck on the cheek, not the passionate kiss which had marked their briefest and most prosaic partings. During the evening meal, he hardly spoke, answering her remarks only in monosyllables, and when, as was their custom on these hot nights, they went for a while out on to the pavement under the veranda, he was so silent that she feared she must have offended him in some way. She hardly dared to ask what was wrong, but in the end, it was he who explained.

"For years," he said, bitterly and slowly, "I've regarded Inspector Burke as a fine fellow, but if I could turn the clock back to this morning and change the day so that he had not called, I would be the happiest man alive!"

He had been standing looking out into the darkness, but now he paced back and forth restlessly, pausing once to lean over and touch her right hand.

"What do you know about my first marriage?" he demanded.

"Very little, Simon." Yet, in her mind, she could hear Aunt Dorcas disparaging this man, and talking of scandal, and most extraordinarily, almost siding with the faithless wife.

"I was too young when I married. Our parents were old friends, you know, but for all that, I hardly knew her, and she hardly knew me, but she was very pretty, and out in the bush, especially in the days before the gold rushes brought so many new people to this country, one didn't meet many pretty, well brought up, girls. My sister became engaged to Caleb Parker, and Sarah, I think, wished to be the same, engaged, I mean. I thought I was in love, but how could I understand such things? I was too green, too inexperienced. It did not take me long to learn that I'd married a shallow, silly, hard-hearted, little flirt. When Dolly was born, she had barely any interest in the child, except as a burden. Then gold was discovered, and our homestead, a few miles out from Sandhurst, was almost immediately surrounded by claims and diggings. You can't imagine how this influenced Sarah! Poor, silly woman. So many men, so much admiration and interest! To make matters worse, many of the men I employed rushed off to dig for gold, so that I had scarcely time to eat and sleep, let alone pander to her whims. She was by now expecting our second child, but this did not stop her from engaging in flirtation after flirtation. Rather to my relief, my wife's twin brother James — you have not met him, for he has now settled in New Zealand — joined us. I hoped, idiot that I was, that her brother would protect her from her own folly. Alas, my brother-in-law was, and probably still is, of as unsteady a nature as was Sarah. While I was absent, he brought to our homestead a young man he had met at the nearby diggings, and when I returned, it was to discover that the three of them had gone off to the mountains to a new rush, taking with them our little daughter, Dolly. Oh, Jane, now that I've found such happiness with you, I can hardly bear to talk of what followed, but you must know if you are to understand. I'd hoped that the whole past was buried, especially as Jim Parker — and how unlike Caleb he is — has left this country!

"I could think only of my poor little Dolly snatched away into a situation, not only immoral, but rough and wild, for that particular rush was into some of the most rugged country in the whole of this colony of Victoria. Of course, I didn't know immediately where they had gone, and several weeks elapsed before I found Sarah and my child. By this time, the birth of our son was imminent, and when I finally tracked down Sarah I was horrified. I'll admit that the home I'd provided wasn't as grand as Curwood, but it was a comfortable timber house which I intended to replace with one of stone as soon as labour was more available. Now I found my wife and little daughter — both Jim and her lover were absent when I arrived — living in the most appalling conditions, in the crudest shack of bark and canvas. It was well into winter, and there was snow on the ground, and icicles hung from the trees and from the roof of that awful little hut. She cried out in fear when she saw me, and fought to stop me going inside. There, on a rough bed, I saw poor little Dolly, coughing out her heart. I was beside myself with rage. Sarah sprang at me, but I pushed her aside and took up Dolly, wrapping her in a blanket, and holding her against me, I rode as quickly as possible down past the snow line into the lower country where it was not quite so cold.

"Dolly was very sick, but thanks to my sister Lucy, she was nursed back to health. Then, Jim Parker arrived with a coarse, drunken woman in tow. This was the wet nurse who was suckling my son, for Sarah had died in childbirth. Jim, of course, made out to Caleb that he had gone off with Sarah and Jack Tallence, her lover, out of a sense of brotherly duty. He always had a glib tongue! He told Caleb and Lucy that Tallence had decided to return to California, where he had spent some time before coming to Australia to look for gold. For my own part, I didn't trust myself to speak to Jim.

"My parents were dead by then, and I felt that there was nothing to keep me here. I sold up, and went to England. As you know, Dolly's health didn't adjust to the climate, and for a while, I feared that her lungs had been permanently damaged during her stay at that mining camp up in the mountains."

"But what has this to do with Inspector Burke's visit?" asked Jane, who had been sitting very quietly, watching heat lightning far away on the horizon without seeing it.

How wrong Aunt Dorcas had been about Simon, and now that she had heard the full story, she did not doubt that

James Parker, the shiftless twin brother, was responsible for talk which had cast aspersions upon Sandford's character. And no wonder that Dolly was, at times, such a strange little girl. Her infant mind must have been bewildered to the point of scarring by her experiences.

Even as she put the question, she could feel her love pouring out towards her husband.

"While you were out of the room for a few minutes," he said very slowly, "Inspector Burke had a few private words with me. Out in the Whipstick, they've found a heap of odds and ends, clothing, camping gear, and the like, marked with Tallence's name. Someone out shooting found them, near a dried out water hole. The things were under some bushes, as if hidden, and very rotted. A police trooper and a black tracker searched the whole area, but found nothing else. Now people are remembering the whole story, and it's being said that Tallence disappeared rather suddenly, just before I went to England."

"Perhaps he sold his possessions before he went back to California." This was said brightly, for she wished to reassure him.

"I don't know, Jane, dearest. I simply don't know. I only met Tallence once or twice, and at that time, I'd not guessed that he had designs upon my wife. I'd hoped the whole wretched business was forgotten. The last thing I want is for that sort of vicious rumour to take hold and hurt you, and my children."

"Mr. James Parker must know the truth."

"The truth?" He laughed, harshly. "The truth and Jim Parker would make strange bedfellows. He had an almost unhealthy devotion to his twin, Jane, and he bitterly resented it when she married me. To hurt me by encouraging Tallence must have amused him."

He came to her, and knelt down by her chair, guiding her arms about his shoulders.

"Jane, now you can understand why I hesitated to court you on board the *Kincardine*. At first, I thought you as shallow a flirt as my poor Sarah. I put the worst interpretation upon our first meeting. Then, gradually, I realised your true character, and knew that whatever the explanation of that episode when you asked me to help you dodge an unwelcome suitor, it was entirely innocent. Oh Jane, dearest, please pray that this business about Tallence will blow over."

There was one instant when Jane longed to tell him the truth about Evan Whiteside, that tenacious persecutor who had so saddened her father's last weeks. Then she recalled her father's dying instructions. She must take the wonderful chance of a new life, and never look back. Even Whiteside belonged in that difficult and poverty hounded world she had left behind, and there he must stay. So, before words could gather on her tongue, she laid her soft cheek against Simon's dark hair. It hurt her terribly to see him in such distress, but at the same time, there was a tiny inner exultation. No more would that little rustling ghost run up the stairs in front of her, or flit amidst the trees in the garden, reminding Jane that Simon's first wife had been a girl in this very house.

She, plain Jane Terrill, had survived

all kinds of difficulty to come into this wonderful state of love and being loved. With her kisses, she would erase her husband's unhappiness. Yet, it was not quite enough. After a while, he drew away, and returned to the subject of Tallence.

"How did his possessions come to be found not ten miles from Curwood?" he demanded. "How? And where is he, Jane? They're trying to make out now that he is dead. They can't think that I killed him. No! They can't."

However, there was too much to be done for much time spent worrying about malicious gossip. The children were expected within a few days. It was still very hot and dry, but their accommodation was ready, and they would travel up from Melbourne on the coach, under the care of their governess. Two days before their anticipated arrival, Sandford decided to ride across country to inspect that property in which he had become interested. She remonstrated that it was a very hot morning, but he smiled as he kissed her goodbye.

"I'm a man of pride, my sweet Jane," he whispered. "You mustn't expect me to remain happy managing my wife's affairs. I'll most likely stay overnight, so don't worry if I'm not back by sunset."

She felt miserable as she watched him ride away on his horse, Bevis, and a little frightened. Already, she had been well drilled in what to do if that scourge of Australian summers, bushfire, should threaten, but fears closed in on her. For Jane, Curwood had been a dream of refuge, but already, she was suspecting that she was not really suited to coping with life in an uncivilised context, and that feeling of helplessness, which had almost overcome her when she had first arrived at the homestead, almost overwhelmed her. She needed Simon so much!

About halfway down the slope to the river, on the track which led to the ford upstream, he turned and waved, and after returning the salute, she went inside in a melancholy frame of mind. She would be glad, she decided, when the children came. At least, then she would not suffer from this loneliness whenever Simon had to be absent.

Lily, who was sensitive enough to keep out of the way when Sandford was home, now emerged boldly, ready to pass on gossip and express her opinions. Officially, she was taking up some freshly ironed clothes, but as Jane came in, she stopped, glad of the chance to resume, briefly, their old footing.

Things would be quiet with Mr. Sandford gone, she remarked, and then went on to comment that they did not have many visitors, but she supposed things would change as they all settled in. That Inspector Burke who'd called the other day, now, he'd seemed a fine gentleman in spite of the queer way he dressed. Of course, there was a bit of talk of him out at the back of the house. He had made a fool of himself, they said, over an actress who'd been touring the goldfields towns. A respectable actress, mind you, but on the stage nevertheless, and Inspector Burke had lost his head over her like any stagestruck schoolboy.

Jane would not have been human if she had not found this mild scandal interesting, but Simon's distress over Burke's private conversation with him, regarding that mysterious find out in the Whipstick, was very much in her mind. She did not doubt that the servants and the station hands were already cognisant of the story. She had quickly learned of the amazing speed with which stories could spread in these comparatively unpopulated areas, and she did not wish her own reactions to be part of the gossip. Tales which began in the public houses of any of the small goldfields settlements scattered through the bush moved along roads with carriers and various itinerants, and were passed on to shepherds, drovers and other pastoral workers over the inevitable campfire with its boiling billycan of tar-black tea. Eventually, these same stories permeated into homesteads through the back door.

"I'm sure that Inspector Burke is capable of managing his own affairs," Jane said, sharply, whilst bracing herself for a remark about the Whipstick discovery.

It did not come. Fortunately, there were barriers which even Lily would not cross. Instead, she veered right off the subject of Inspector Burke.

"Do you know whether the governess, Miss Lamont, is bringing much stuff with her?" she asked. "There's not much place for extra in her room."

"I doubt it. Governesses cannot afford many clothes. Her trunk will have to go out into one of the storerooms if it doesn't fit in."

Snubbed, Lily went on upstairs, and on impulse, Jane took up her widebrimmed hat, and went outdoors again. The air hardly stirred, and she dabbed at her damp forehead with her handkerchief.

She thought, I'll find a shady spot on the river bank, and she began walking down the long, gentle slope, in much the same direction her husband had taken not half an hour previously. Rather illogically, the coming of the governess, Miss Lamont, began to worry her. When she had received Lucy Parker's letter telling her of the woman's excellent recommendations and experience, Jane had felt relieved. Now she wished that Lucy had chosen someone younger, for she dreaded that Miss Lamont might find

Lily, close to her own age, congenial.

I should follow Simon's advice and send Lily packing, she told herself, but then that streak of softheartedness took over. Lily had stayed with her when she was sick, and through those dreadful first days here at Curwood — and besides, she was so good at things domestic.

Jane did not walk all the way to the ford, but left the track about three hundred yards from the homestead. The grass was only a brown stubble, already cropped to the ground by sheep which had been let loose here some weeks before. It was the easiest way, said Simon, to nullify the fire hazard between the homestead and the river.

The river itself was much reduced from the torrent it had been in spring, and moved quietly and shallowly over rounded rocks from one deep pool to another. Blessedly, not one trace of gold had ever been found here, so that trees and shrubbery still remained to line its banks, and she found a suitably shady spot.

I should be hard at work supervising the household, she reprimanded herself, but she leaned over and soaked her handkerchief in the cool water, and wiped her face with it. She had so many problems. One expected that wealth would remove one from all mundane worries, but the life she had led with Papa had not prepared her for a life of chatelaine. Sooner or later, she and Simon would have to entertain on the scale expected of well-to-do graziers. How would she cope?

She was forcing her mind on to this channel. All the while, errantly, her thoughts went back to Simon's shock over the find out there in the Whipstick wilderness.

However, at the same time, the cool water provided an irresistible lure. There was no one about, not even a stray sheep, and she slipped off her shoes and stockings, and sitting on the edge of the bank, hitched up her skirts and dangled her feet in the water. Oh, how refreshing it was. Just as in bed on a chilly night, one's whole body shivered if one's feet were cold — as Jane knew only too well from lodgings where blankets were thin and coal grudgingly supplied — the

144

converse was true. On a very hot day, chilling one's feet had the effect of reducing the all-over temperature.

After ten minutes or so, she unwillingly decided that such self-indulgence must cease. She really felt much more able to face the rest of a long day without Simon, but as she pulled her feet up out of the water, she had a nasty surprise. Several leeches had attached themselves to her white skin.

She was engaged in the highly unpleasant task of removing them when, out of the corner of her eye, she saw a shadow on the ground at her side. A man's shadow.

"I'm sorry if I startled you, Mrs. Sandford. It is Mrs. Sandford, isn't it?"

She managed to pull her skirts down over her bare legs and feet, very embarrassed at being caught in such a state, and looked upwards. The sun was shining directly into her eyes, and she had to shade them with her hand to see whom the man might be. The voice was not familiar, but she knew the face.

8

IT was not a handsome face, being too
thin and aquiline, and the lower part
was concealed by a neatly trimmed
light brown beard. The eyes were very
blue, and of a piercing hardness.

"I'll look the other way for a few
moments," he said, in a clipped, totally
unamused voice.

Jane could not move for several
seconds. This was the man she had
seen at Station Pier on the day the
Kincardine had berthed, the man whose
look of hatred for Simon Sandford had
so impressed her that he had returned in
a dream with her old foe, Evan Whiteside.
Then, remembering her dignity, she
hastily pulled on stockings and shoes,
and he proferred a hand to help her to
her feet. For a moment, she wished to
refuse the assistance, but the alternative
was an unseemly scramble, as she was
still perched on the edge of the bank.

"They told me at the house that

you had last been seen walking towards the river," he explained. "Oh, I forgot. Forgive me, Mrs. Sandford. We haven't been introduced."

All the time, as he spoke in that sharp, unemotional voice which so matched those cold blue eyes, she knew that he was regarding her minutely, right down to the wet handkerchief in her left hand. The leeches had left smarting spots on her legs, and she was uneasily aware of the dirt and grass clinging to her wide gingham skirts.

"I'm James Parker," he announced, without further preamble. "I've had business in the vicinity, and I decided to call in the hope of seeing my niece and nephew. However, I've found out that they haven't arrived yet."

"We're expecting them on Thursday," she said, in a flat voice. While she tried to compose herself, to present an indifferent face to her husband's treacherous former brother-in-law, she was astonished to find out that he was quite tall. Like many men of slender build, his height was deceptive.

"I was under the impression, Mr.

Parker, that you now resided in New Zealand," she continued, coolly.

"I've taken up land on the Canterbury Plains, out of Christchurch in the South Island," he nodded. "But I've a few loose ends here in Victoria which have to be tied up. Once that is done, I'll live there permanently. I've been faced with the necessity of crossing the Tasman Sea several times over the past few years, Mrs. Sandford, and believe me, it can be a very rough passage."

By now, they were walking back towards the homestead, and despite her instinctive fear and dislike of the man, she was determined to keep up this flow of small talk.

"You must find Curwood very changed, Mr. Parker," she said, whilst her mind struggled with the coincidence of the man's arrival here so soon after Simon had learnt of that eerie find out in the desolate Whipstick.

For the first time, there was a flash of expression on that cold and sculptured face. It was amusement, but of a detached, almost cynical variety, which left her wondering how much of it was

148

directed against her.

"Changed? In some ways yes, in others, no. The land is still the same, so gentle-looking, but so ferocious underneath. We survived the great fire on Black Thursday back in 1851, Mrs. Sandford, by sitting in that very pool where you were dangling your feet. Miraculously, the fire skirted the house, but our outbuildings and most of our stock went. We had no option but to sell out to your grandfather, who had plenty of capital from his coal mining and other interests. My brother Caleb, who has a good head for business, also helped our battered fortunes by doing well down in Melbourne during the first days of the gold rush. As you've probably heard, our parents decided to join the Wakefield scheme for colonising the South Island in New Zealand, and I soon decided that I preferred the bitter winters there to the chance of being roasted alive here in Victoria."

All the time he was speaking, she sensed that he was sizing her up, not assessing her as a young woman, but rather judging her intelligence and attitudes.

"It's a shame that Simon is away today," she said, deliberately guileless.

"I'm sure that Simon must have mentioned me to you," he returned, holding open the picket gate for her. "I didn't want to see Simon, and I'm sure he doesn't wish to see me. I wanted to assure myself that the children are happy."

The significance of the last was not lost on her.

"Believe me, Mr. Parker," she stated, as acidly as she could, "that I've no intention of being a wicked stepmother."

For the first time, his self-possession was dented.

"I'm sorry," he replied, quite gently. "I was tactless, and I must apologise."

He refused her offer of a midday meal, saying that he had to be on his way, and after a cool drink, he mounted his nondescript hired horse and rode away, ramrod backed, and leaving her prey to all kinds of fancy.

She had no doubt whatsoever that Parker's expressed desire to see his small niece and nephew was a piece of pure deception. He was, she was positive, sniffing out the lay of the land,

150

trying to discover whether the new Mrs. Sandford was as foolish and as easily led into the abyss as his late sister. If he had arrived recently in Melbourne from New Zealand, he must have spoken with his brother and learned that the children were not yet at Curwood. Mr. Parker's sophistry was obvious, and not very clever. Papa could have summed up Mr. Parker quite aptly.

"They do but flatter with their lips and dissemble in their double hearts."

Hopefully, the result of this would be:

"Whoso diggeth a pit shall fall therein."

Simon Sandford's reaction to the information that James Parker had made a brief call was much as she expected. He was furious.

"If I'd been here, I'd have taken pleasure in ordering him off," he fumed. "What insolence! After all the trouble he caused me in times past. You're right, Jane. He must have known that the children weren't here. What else did he have to say for himself?"

Her cheeks coloured slightly as she recalled the undignified circumstances in which Parker had found her.

"Oh, only a few generalities about New Zealand."

"H'm." Simon stood with his back to her, staring out moodily into the night from the edge of the veranda, puffing silently on his cigar for some moments. When he replied, it was with a complete change of subject. "I'll be taking up the Omega place late in March, Jane. It'll mean some changes for us, unfortunately, until things are settled to my liking. I'll have to travel back and forth for a while. That doesn't please me, but I can see no alternative. The homestead over there is very small, and in any case, too much has been spent on this house for us to wish to move so soon. You know that it was always my intention to invest in a property of my own, Jane. That is why I called here on that day to find you in such trouble with that snake!"

He turned, and came to her side, stroking her hair softly with his free hand.

"Omega is ideal for what I have in mind, dearest. I want to specialise in stud work, Jane, improving sheep breeds, and

Omega is more suitable than Curwood. The land is flatter, and the soil is richer. Oh, don't look so sad! I'm not going on a voyage round the world. It's only twelve miles away."

★ ★ ★

The children's arrival brought with it another surprise, and one which, coupled with James Parker's recent visit, set Jane thinking very seriously about the Parker family's motives. Something which she now decided was that although Lucy was Simon's sister, she was subservient to anything decided by her husband and brother-in-law.

The governess was not the Miss Lamont they had expected. Instead of a steady, fortyish woman wearing the lace-edged cap of maturity, the person who had accompanied the children up from Melbourne was no more than twenty four, with a head of fair curling hair which no amount of centre parting and smoothing down could subdue. As well, she possessed mischievous blue eyes, and an English rose complexion, rather a rarity amongst the Australian born. Her name was Chloris McFarlane, and she was first cousin to Caleb and James Parker on their mother's side.

Her explanation was simple, and verified in a letter from Lucy. Miss Lamont had fallen prey to colonial fever[1], and was not expected to be able to resume her duties for about three months. Therefore, as Chloris's own employment as governess had recently terminated when her young charges had been sent out to school, she had taken over the job on a temporary basis, for she was to be married in May.

Despite the twinges of suspicion that Miss Lamont's illness had provided a convenient opportunity to place a spy at Curwood, in case Jane turned out to be an unsuitable mother, she found Chloris extremely agreeable. She was cheerful, lively, and competent with the children. Dolly was still the same difficult little girl, apt to withdraw into a world of her own, or throw horrific tantrums if

---

[1] Typhoid fever

things did not go her way, but Chloris had patience, and a shrewd knowledge of the childish mind.

Rodney, far more placid in nature, soon slipped into the way of calling Jane Mama. Dolly called her nothing, and no prompting would force her, until a confrontation one afternoon which brought matters to a head.

"Stepmother!" said Dolly, in a taunting tone which left no doubt as to her meaning.

Dolly went off to bed in disgrace, but this did not remedy the second Mrs. Sandford's hurt.

"Do I seem as wicked as all that?" asked Jane, in a despairing voice, as she and her husband prepared to go to bed under the white netting which protected them from mosquitoes in the continuing hot and humid weather.

"Wicked? You? Oh, Jane!" He bent down over her as she sat before her dressing table, plaiting her brown hair, and he kissed the back of her neck. "Dolly has always been a stubborn child. Give her more time, and speak firmly to Chloris about it. I hesitate to say this, because I know you like her, but I can't help wondering whether she is encouraging Dolly to remember her mother. The child should have forgotten by now."

"Why should Miss McFarlane do such a thing? She and I get along extremely well."

"She hero-worshipped Jim Parker when she was younger, in her middle teens."

"But she's engaged to be married, and from what I can gather, very much in love."

"They're cousins, remember. Jim could always twist Chloris about his little finger. It would amuse Jim to see you cast in the role of wicked stepmother."

Jane could not bring herself to reply. She remembered only too well how she had so sharply told Mr. Parker that she had no intention of being a wicked stepmother. Had she put the idea into his mind, and had he in turn passed it on to Chloris? She shuddered.

"Now," said Simon, hands on her shoulders, "what was that for?"

"Oh, Simon!" She turned on her stool, and reached up to him. "Why should they begrudge you your new life and happiness? I can't help thinking . . . feeling . . . that what Inspector Burke told you about finding those things out in the Whipstick was connected with James Parker's visit. I do like Chloris. She is such good company when you are away at Omega, but do you think we should send her away? Simon, I couldn't bear it if things went wrong for us. Before he died, Papa told me not to look back, but sometimes, I can't help it. I remember how poor we were, and how insecure our lives were. You've never been really poor, Simon. It's far worse than not having enough to eat, or living in horrid lodgings, or putting cardboard into one's shoes to try to keep out the wet. It's the fighting to keep one's dignity and one's pride. And it's being lonely. For people like us, Simon, it was the loneliness which was so unbearable. We couldn't mix with the low and coarse, who resented us, and no one else wanted us. To have security, and love, and a home! Oh, how wonderful it is! Please, please, please, don't let anything change it."

"Never," he whispered, passionately.

"You'll never, never have to remember that life again. We won't let it happen, dearest one."

Much later, she lay awake still whilst he slept. It was, to her, stifling under the netting, and she arose and went to the window, and looked out across a scene black and white in the moonlight. It was the same window from which, in her nightmare, she had seen Evan Whiteside and James Parker (whom she had not known by name at that time) and the great owl. Tonight, the garden, tidied by a quiet Chinese Simon had hired, was not quite the untidy maze it had been, and although it was still far from being the miniature English landscape upon which she had set her heart, there were signs of the order to come. She could see something on one of the gateposts, solid, jar-shaped. Then it spread its wings and fluttered away heavily, uttering the eerie cry of an owl.

She forced back a little cry, and made herself think reasonably. Why am I like this, she asked herself, forever creating Gothic tales out of nothing?

In years to come, she would look

back on it, and wonder, for like her sad memories of her wandering life with Papa, it would be part of the past. Yet, she could not deny this sense of foreboding, of something not right. At this period of her life, her instincts against danger were finely honed, warning her against . . . what?

It was easy to dismiss this strange sense of peril as a result of nervousness occasioned by the grief of losing both her father and her new-found relatives within a few months. Years later, very occasionally, in the course of her happy and active life, she would pause and puzzle.

She could never claim to have 'the sight', but for a while, as some animals seem able to perceive coming disaster, she had this almost constant edginess, and even the embraces and comforting common sense of her adored husband could not dismiss her uneasiness.

9

FEW of the trees in the Curwood orchard bore much fruit that season. As Sandford had pointed out on the occasion of his first visit, years of neglect had taken their toll, and the few plums which did appear were quickly ruined by flocks of noisy parrots brought hither by that extraordinary telepathy which guides birds to a change of diet. There were a few apples, but they were miserably small, and most were spoiled by codlin moth.

Hope now rested with the three fig trees which, apparently, had thrived on neglect and were carrying good crops. The Chinese gardener caught, and killed, a few parrots, and dangled these gruesomely from miniature gallows — trees on the upper branches. The marauders were impressed, and Jane began to have high hopes of fresh fruit and fig jam, which Lily promised to make.

Then Roddy ran inside to cry out that there was a big boy stealing figs. Dolly was at her lessons with Chloris McFarlane, and Jane hurried out with Lily close behind. Rodney was right. There was a big boy picking figs, two big boys in fact, barefooted, patched urchins, who were putting the fruit into a battered basket.

"Who are you?"

The elder and larger of the two turned. He was about fifteen, spindly built, but towering over short Jane and Lily.

"An' what's it to yer?" he demanded, in that nasal whine which Jane had already discovered as belonging to the native born Australian lower orders.

"You are taking the figs without permission!". she snapped, standing very straight.

"And 'oo might yer be?"

"I happen to be Mrs. Sandford."

"Well, we allus comes in Mr. Wheeler's time to git a few figs for the kinchen, and we don't see how's things 'ave changed."

The younger did have the grace to look furtive, but the older boy had

161

already learned that cold cheek often wins the day.

What he did not expect was that little Mrs. Sandford, for all her youth and demure looks, was not without experience in dealing with his kind.

"Kinchen! Don't use that thieves' cant with me! Whose children? I see no children."

"'E means our little brudders and sisters," muttered the younger one, who was, she judged, about thirteen. "We didn't mean no 'arm, Mrs. Sandford. We thoughts it was still orright. I'm Tom Wells from down the track a bit, and that's George."

Jane thought of the dreadful shack, the hideous flume dominating the valley, and her heart softened. A basket of fruit would be a treat for the small Wells children, of whom there seemed to be a tribe. Still, George was an insolent whelp, bound for a bad end, and she would not give in to his intimidation.

"You'd best leave," she said, quietly, and after some shifting from one foot to the other, the two youths stalked away, leaving behind their basket and the fruit.

She allowed an hour to pass, and then ordered the small cart harnessed up. By this time, Dolly's lessons were over for the day, and accompanied by Chloris, who was more experienced in handling the reins than herself, Jane set out for the Wells establishment, the basket of figs on board. It was high time, she said to Chloris, that she made some sort of neighbourly gesture to Mrs. Wells.

"Poor thing," mused Chloris. "I can't imagine a worse fate than living as she does, in that little shack with all those children. Still, they must be bringing gold out of that mine, or they wouldn't stay on. I remember my cousin Jim saying how very beautiful that valley was once, with tall trees and those marvellous man-ferns down at the bottom. It was partly burnt out in the great fire on Black Thursday, and then the miners moved in and completely ruined it."

She stopped the horse on the dusty track at the point nearest the shack, and the two young women sat for a few moments looking down into the devastated valley.

"A habitation of dragons, and a court

for owls," murmured Jane, without thinking, and Chloris laughed.

"I don't know about dragons, but Jim said there were tiger snakes near the creek, and they're quite dangerous enough! As for the owls, poor things, their big trees have all gone."

She hero-worshipped James Parker, Simon had said. Oh, don't be so silly, Jane Sandford, she chided herself, silently. Chloris is exactly what she seems, a bright, unaffected young woman with no plotting on her mind except plans for her wedding.

There was a slippery, precarious path down from the road to the shack, and the girls had to cling to one another to make the descent without mishap. The mine and puddling machine, worked round and round by a tired and sway-backed horse, were not as near to the shack as had appeared from the rocks high above the other side of the valley.

Both Jane and Chloris paused to look with considerable curiosity at the extraordinary and makeshift contrivances which helped the Wells family in their own fight for survival. The water from the flume was their life support during this long summer season. After being carried across the valley from the spring below the high rocks, it was distributed two ways by wooden gutters, one lot of water coming down into the puddling machine to wash through the dirt brought out from the mine, so that the speaks of gold could be separated from the rest of the muddy sludge. The remainder was directed into channels which irrigated the Wells' vegetable patch and provided water for their cows, goats and flock of fowls, all of which looked as wild and scraggy as the horde of Wells juveniles who now came from every direction to inspect the visitors.

Two men emerged from the mine tunnel, which burrowed straight into the side of the hill, one trundling a large barrow of dirt and shale, and the other carrying a large shovel. They both stopped dead, and one, the barrow pusher, Jane saw out of the corner of her eye, a slightish man with a red beard, let go of the handles and hurried back into the shelter of the mine.

The other man immediately laid his

shovel on the dirt in the barrow and pushed the heavy load to the puddling machine, where he stopped the plodding horse, and then diverted the water splashing down by turning away the bottom part of the gutter, which was apparently on a sort of hinge. The water ran down the slope along a deeply eroded rut into a dirty pond below. This pond was also the Wells rubbish tip, and as the fresh jet of water hit the surface, a large cloud of insects arose.

"'Ullo, 'ullo, what do you want?"

This was the man coming forward, wiping the palms of his hands on his filthy and patched moleskin trousers.

"We've brought some figs for Mrs. Wells and the children," said Jane. Poor, wild, little things, she added silently, as the younger ones darted away, too shy to stay for long under the scrutiny of strangers.

"We keeps ourselves to ourselves 'ere," said Mr. Wells, who was easily identified by his close resemblance to all the young ones, and most particularly to George Wells, of whom there was no sign. "We don't want nothin' to do with youse squatters."

"I'd think we'd best put down the basket and go," whispered Chloris.

"Your sons left your basket behind," stated Jane, in a loud and clear voice, thinking, so much for benign and Christian gestures. "I found the boys in our orchard. There seems to have been a misunderstanding of some kind, and as there are plenty of figs, I can see no reason why your family shouldn't enjoy some."

Mr. Wells brooded over this for a short time. He was, it was plain to see, the sort of man who had long ago taken to heart the ancient injunction about bewaring of Greeks bearing gifts. He eyed the basket of figs as if sure it contained an asp.

"We don't want no charity from your kind," he snarled, and took a threatening step forward. "Youse squatters are agin us workin' men. You don't want us to 'ave the land we'se as entitled to as your sort."

There was only one answer, instant and dignified retreat. At the top of the steep and slippery slope, with its scraps of shale stuttering down behind the girls, both stopped for breath and glanced back. The whole brood of Wells offspring were eating figs, and Mr. Wells was pushing one into his mouth as he returned to his labours.

Chloris and Jane looked at each other, and then staggered back to their vehicle, both half bent over with laughter.

"I hope they saved some for Mrs. Wells and the other man," remarked Jane as their mirth died down, and the horse trotted sedately back to Curwood homestead.

"So do I. Poor woman! But, what other man? I didn't see another man. I think Tom and George were keeping out of our sight on purpose, but they were out quickly enough for their share of the fruit as soon as our backs were turned."

"You must have seen him. He came out of the mine with Mr. Wells and then hurried back. He was quite slight, and had a red beard."

"I didn't see him," replied Chloris. "Are you sure it wasn't one of the older boys?"

"Not unless George or Tom has grown a beard within the past two hours," answered Jane.

Chloris shrugged.

"Your eyes must be sharper than mine," she said.

So, the incident was dismissed, but later it was to take on far greater importance.

"Those poor children," continued Chloris. "Growing up almost like little savages. Worse, perhaps, because my father had quite an association with the blacks at one time, and however they appear to our civilised eyes, the young ones are carefully educated into their ways and religion. But when I see our own young children allowed to grow up without schooling of any kind, I feel so hopeless and helpless."

"You and my father would have found much in common," said Jane, a little surprised at this show of feeling in Chloris. It also reminded her how little she actually knew about her stepchildren's governess. She was Dolly's and Rodney's cousin once removed, but had come to Curwood without references or any

169

kind of the recommendations usual in the employment of a governess.

"Ah, was he also determined to set the world to rights?"

Chloris's voice became light and merry again, as if she were a little wary of showing the other side of her nature again.

"Yes. And I'm afraid that he was not very successful," replied Jane.

The mail had arrived during their absence, picked up at the nearest township by one of the men. There were several businesslike letters for Simon, three for Chloris, one addressed to the children from their Aunt Lucy, to be read out by an adult, and one for Jane, carrying a New South Wales postage stamp.

It was a packet rather than a letter, carrying the name Miss Jane Terrill, care of the hotel where she had stayed during her illness, and forwarded by the proprietor of that establishment.

With some curiosity, she tore apart the seal and opened out the wrapping. This stiff paper carried a brief letter on its reverse side, neatly written in an unfamiliar and slightly immature hand,

170

as if the person who had inscribed it was not used to holding a pen. The actual contents comprised a stained envelope, stampless, with its address so blurred and watermarked that it took her some moments to decipher it as being addressed to herself at the same destination as on the outside of the packet.

'Dear Miss Terrill,' read the letter. 'Whilst walking along the shore near my home, I found the enclosed letter wedged between rocks under the shelter of a larger rock. I have therefore taken the liberty of sending it on to you. Yrs. fthly., B. Watson.'

There was no return address on the missive, and no date. Mr. B. Watson apparently did not desire to enter into further correspondence.

The other letter was from Uncle Hugh MacBride, written on board the *Kincardine* during the last minutes before the ship crashed into the cliffs.

Lily came in with tea.

"Mrs. Sandford," she said, anxiously, "are you feeling all right?"

Jane was standing in the middle of the

big room, dazedly holding the letter in a limp hand at her side. Her head was whirling, her throat choked with disbelief. The writing, smudged from immersion, was hard to read, but still sufficiently distinct for each word to be deciphered.

'My dear Jane,' it began, 'You may be surprised to receive a letter from myself rather than from your aunt, but believe me, my dear, it is only with the utmost unwillingness that I have decided to write these lines.

'We will be in Sydney before morning, and in the bussle of arriving and settling in again, I shall have little time, so I am taking advantage of these last hours at sea.

'First of all, it is my hope that your health has improved and that you will soon join us in Sydney.

'The reason for this letter is simple, to warn you against the man Sandford. I am not blind, my dear, and saw that you had developed certain feelings towards Mr. Sandford. Your aunt has formed one of her dislikes for him, although I have always found him pleasant. It has been a hard dicision for me, but for your sake, I am parsing on what is most likely pure slander. Remember, my dear, there is a saying, where there is smoke there is fire.

'Talk about Melbourne has it that Sandford was a fool to come back. His wife's paramoor, Jack Tallance, disappeared in rather strange circumstances, and there's a suspicion that Sandford took the law into his own hands.

'Follow your aunt's good council, my dear, and don't have anything to do with the man. There are plenty of splendid young fellows waiting for you here in Sydney.

'With best wishes for your improving health,

Hugh MacBride.'

In the blank way that one does after a shock, she thought, poor Uncle Hugh made some silly spelling mistakes. And then she heard Lily's voice, and felt Lily's arm about her shoulders.

"You'd best lie down and rest, Mrs. Sandford. They say it passes after the first few months, though I don't recall

173

Mrs. MacBride ever being poorly."

You fool, thought Jane, but she did not resist. I'm not having a baby, or if I am, I don't know about it.

She suffered herself to be led upstairs, to have her hoops and stays removed, and to lie down on her big white quilted bed.

"Do you want the smelling salts?"

She whispered that she wished only to be left alone for a while. The letter lay on the dressing table, and she wanted to rise up and take it and tear it into shreds. It was a foul thing, as horrible as if it had risen from the putrefaction of the mass grave into which the *Kincardine*'s victims had been buried.

Later, she heard Sandford arrive home. The children were immediately all about him, competing for his attention, as children do after their father has been absent for even so short a period as two days. He must have been told that his wife was unwell, because he hurried up the stairs, heavily, still wearing his riding boots, and she could even hear the faint jingle of his spurs.

"My dearest, what's wrong? You've

been out in the sun without a hat!"

She did not reply immediately, but lay still, her head propped up on the pillows, whilst she scrutinised him as if seeing him for the first time. He was a fine looking man, by any standards, and instead of the pallor of their earliest meetings, he now had a well-tanned skin from spending most of the summer out of doors. It added enormously to his physical attraction, and the air of dark romance, which inexplicably in such an essentially practical man, was part of his being.

"There's a letter," she said, faintly. "On the dressing table. It's from Hugh MacBride, I want you to read it."

"Hugh MacBride!" His perplexity was immense.

"Yes. It was washed ashore and lay under a rock for months until it was found by a person called Watson who happened to be walking that way. Please, Simon, read it. You must."

He picked it up, and unfolded the two stained sheets of paper, and as he read, she watched him closely. At first, there was no reaction but a tightening of the lips, but at the end, he flung it down in a fury, and then buried his face in his hands.

"Oh, my God!" he cried. "Is there no end to it? Oh, my dearest Jane, if only I could have spared you this." Then he came and sat by her on the bed, and took both her hands in his, and looked deeply into her own eyes. "Do you think I'm a murderer? Is that what you think of me?"

"No, Simon. I could never think such a thing of you. But what right has anyone to spread such stories?"

"They've done it well. Well enough to send an old friend here to ask if I knew anything about some old clothes found out in the bush. No wonder . . . oh never mind."

She was now the one to do the comforting. She sat up and put her arms about his neck and drew his head down against her breasts.

"What mustn't I mind?" she murmured, stroking his dark hair.

"Down in Melbourne — I'd noticed it. Fellows I've known for years acting as if they'd rather not know me."

"Simon, on the day we first arrived in Melbourne, I saw James Parker walking towards your group on the wharf. You were with Lucy and Caleb and" here she hesitated a second, for she still hated the sound of her rival's name, "Mrs. O'Brien."

"Oh, yes, I remember. Mrs. O'Brien somehow invited herself into my family group." The hint of amusement in his voice was very reassuring and reaffirmed her knowledge that it was Mrs. O'Brien who had done all the running. "Jim Parker did turn up. He'd known of course that I was returning to Australia — Lucy and Caleb had received my letters advising them of it weeks before." The amusement had quite vanished and was replaced by a heavy grimness. "He did his work well."

"Simon, I noticed him especially on that day. I did not know then whom he might be, but I'd never in my life seen such hatred on a human face. But why should people believe him? You told me yourself that Jack Tallence had returned to California. Surely it is easy enough to prove."

"Jane, Melbourne's grown enormously since the beginning of the gold rush, but it's still the same little town it used to be at heart. There's an element in this world of ours which'd rather think the worst of a man than the best."

Jane was feeling better now, and her mind was working with a forced clarity. The affair had to be cleared up, for his sake, for hers, and for that of the children, and she told him so.

"You must see Inspector Burke again and insist that he goes right to the bottom of it. If James Parker is responsible, he must be stopped, and I hope, punished."

He stood up, and looked down at her, a slight, almost enigmatic, smile crooking his mouth.

"What did I do to deserve such a loyal wife?" he murmured, half to himself. And then, in a louder tone: "Jane, you've heard of the lady who protested too much. I think that sooner or later, Mr. Parker will go too far. Then we can deal with him."

"But, Simon, he's already gone to the length of placing clothes out in the bush to help his horrid story. Surely, that is far enough."

"We don't know that, Jane."

That was true, but she knew from the little line between his brows that he was as worried as she was herself.

Later, that same evening, he made the suggestion that they take a few days off and seek out whatever pleasures Sandhurst might have to offer.

10

THE new town of Sandhurst, laid out and created on the site of the Bendigo gold rush, was wealthy from the metal which was being taken, apparently without end, from the many mines in the area.

The name Bendigo had been derived, it was said, from that of a shepherd who had lived in a hut near the spot where the first discoveries were made, this soubriquet being given because of a fancied resemblance to Abednigo, a well-known British pugilist of the time. Perhaps because of the strong liquors which were part of bush life, the name changed to Bendigo, sounding suitably Australian, and fitting in nicely with genuine aboriginal names like Ballarat, Echuca, and the rest.

However, after a short period which saw enormous riches pour out of the settlement's surrounds, the rapidly growing town decided that it deserved some dignity. The name Sandhurst, topical at the time of the Crimean War, was chosen, and for a number of years, the pompous element tried hard to forget that the place was originally called after a common prizefighter. Unfortunately for pride, the great gold discoveries at Bendigo had become famous the world round, the oldtimers still preferred the name anyway, and in the end, Sandhurst was dropped and virtually forgotten.

After the shock of receiving Hugh MacBride's tragically delayed letter, Jane was glad to leave Curwood for a few days. Actually, the purpose of the journey was for Simon to further his plans to take over the Omega run, but he assured his wife that they would try to enjoy themselves and forget the cloud which had settled over their lives.

On the outskirts of Sandhurst, there were still many independent miners seeking the alluvial gold they hoped lay near the surface, staying on beyond sense in the hope of finding a 'jeweller's shop' as rich claims were known. Closer to the town was the settled district, or lands sold to small farmers to provide fresh food for the town dwellers. As Jane already knew, the graziers looked with disfavour upon these settled districts as a hint of things to come, for they were areas which had been reclaimed by the Crown from their own vast peppercorn-rental leaseholds.

Jane and her husband passed the spot where gold had been found at Bendigo for the first time, on the banks of a creek by, it was said, two young Irishwomen filling in time whilst their husbands were otherwise occupied. The district surrounding this site was now called Golden Square, a place of derricks, mullock heaps, small cottages, throbbing donkey engines, stacked firewood and wandering animals. Nearby was the Chinese Camp, a squalid assortment of ram-shackle buildings built one against the other, forked throughout by lanes barely wide enough to allow two men to pass. The Chinese Camp was despised, hated and avoided by the whites.

However, right in town, there were the beginnings of fine buildings, and the general standard of housing was better. These were the homes of people who had come to stay, the merchants, the businessmen, the small tradesmen, and such adjuncts of civilisation as doctors, lawyers and the clergy. In Sandhurst's main street, silk-hatted men gathered to buy and sell shares in the latest boom mine, smart horses drew smart carriages, and crinolined women shopped or went about the essential rites of paying calls.

It was raw, rough about the edges, but with a strange Britishness of atmosphere as the predominant section of the population organised their new lives on the lines of what they had left behind.

Not only excellent and varied shops tempted the visitor: there were theatres in Bendigo, and much of the entertainment was of a high standard, for the best companies toured the larger gold centres as a matter of course. After a quite passable meal at their hotel, Simon Sandford suggested an evening at a nearby theatre.

It worried him, he said gently, that she had been so melancholy since receiving that letter. She was rather tired after their journey, but to please him, she agreed to his proposal.

The play offering was a popular

melodrama which featured a reconstruction of the Siege of Lucknow, very much in everyone's mind with the horrors of the Indian Mutiny still in the immediate past.

During the first few minutes of the first act, some rather boisterous young men, arriving late, took their places in a box overlooking the stage. The audience were a mixed lot, miners and their families, wealthy local magnates, raffish characters male and female, and the stolidly respectable, but they all had one thing in common. The opening lines of the play, announcing the rebellion and all its imminent perils, had grabbed the patrons' attention immediately, and as one body, they resented any interruption.

Several members of the audience hushed and shushed, with a few coarser remarks interpolated. Then, as her own gaze travelled the curve of the front row of the dress circle to the box, Jane saw that one of the noisy quartet was none other than James Parker. To his credit, he was the quietest, and obviously telling his slightly tipsy companions to behave themselves.

Jane had imagined that James Parker had already left the district, if not Australia. To see him here brought about a sensation of anger, and a dismissal of the more cheerful thoughts which had been occupying her. Alongside her, she heard her husband mutter, "Good lord, it's Jim Parker," and she knew that for him, as for her, the evening had been spoiled.

The play was exciting enough, with plenty of sentiment mixed in with the action, as the heroine and her family simultaneously survived the perils of Lucknow and sorted out their problems. When the Scots nursemaid sang 'Annie Laurie' there were demands for an encore. When the faithful Indian servant offered to subsist on the water in which the tiny ration of rice had been boiled so that the children could have his share, tears flowed freely from feminine eyes, and judging by the clearing of throats, many a masculine heart was similarly touched.

At the very nadir of despair on the stage, the Scots nursemaid announced to her disbelieving fellow sufferers that she could hear the skirl of the pipes, and absolute silence held the audience. Everyone knew what was going to happen, but everyone was enthralled by the sheer excitement of one of the best publicised episodes of the Indian Mutiny.

Everyone, with one exception. James Parker sat back indolently, bored and indifferent to the events on the stage.

"I hear-r-d it again! Canna ye hea-r-r it too?"

The actress, wearing a tartan shawl to identify her as of Scots nationality (a rather unlikely touch in tropical India and very trying on a summer's night in Australia), cupped a hand to her ear, and the child in the same scene who had been dying of fever and malnutrition arose on its sickbed and cried out, "I hear them too, Mama! I can hear the bagpipes!"

Off stage, to collaborate this, there was a faint wail of pipes.

Handkerchiefs were now very busy, but just as it seemed that every woman in the audience must be washed away by her own tears, the pipes skirled with increasing volume, and a battered defender of Lucknow, dirty bandage about his head, rushed on to the stage, and cried out that Sir Colin Campbell's relief column was in sight. They were all saved!

The audience clapped and cheered, and the orchestra joined in 'The Campbells are Coming'. This was the moment everyone had expected, and when it came, they enjoyed it to the full.

Yet, although his companions were boisterously applauding, James Parker sat coolly disregarding the near pandemonium which had greeted the climax of the play. Nothing, Jane was sure, as she dabbed at her own eyes, could touch his icy nature. Except hatred for his former brother-in-law.

The Sandfords left the theatre as hurriedly as possible after the final curtain, for without saying a word, they mutually desired to avoid Parker. Back in the hotel bedroom, Jane voiced her thoughts.

"He must be the one who is trying to ruin your good name, Simon. He is quite without feeling. Anyone could see that tonight!"

Sandford managed a rueful laugh.

"Jane, because a man doesn't burst into tears over the goings-on of a lot of actors and actresses he isn't a criminal. Now, dearest, promise me, you'll do your best to stop thinking about Parker and those rumours. The amount of interest you're taking in him and his doings is making me jealous."

But, there was something superficial in his cheerfulness, as if he himself were trying hard to push away the suspicions in his own mind.

When she thought about it later, Jane became sure that Parker, either by following them, or by making enquiries, had discovered where they were staying. Sandford, in the throes of completing his arrangements to take over the Omega run, had an appointment with a bank manager at nine the next morning, and before ten, Jane too went out, a shopping list discreetly tucked into her reticule. With her pretty parasol held high to protect her from the sun's testing heat, she had not gone very far before she wished she had a veil as well, for a stiff northerly had blown up, and the whole town sweltered under a pall of dust as much from the surrounding waste lands left by mining as from the dry interior deserts.

Still, the list had to be fulfilled. Jane had by now discovered that however careful one was in judging what was needed for a fairly isolated household, some things were inevitably overlooked. The kitchen knives, for instance, were a disgrace, left over from the bad old days of Mr. Wheeler's management. They had to be replaced. And just before she left, Chloris McFarlane had reminded her about deficiencies in the schoolroom supplies. Also, Simon had pointed out that although it seemed at present that summer would go on forever, the question of stuffs for the children's winter clothes had to be investigated.

Shopping is always an exhausting business, and when the last errand was completed, Jane resolved to return to her hotel room to rest. Two doors away from her destination, she noticed a well-stocked bookshop, and decided to enquire whether the newest Trollope novel had arrived, for she and Papa had read together, and thoroughly enjoyed,

'The Warden', with its shrewd portrayals of clerical life.

Then, she saw James Parker emerging from the front door of the hotel where she and her husband were staying. Without hesitation, she turned the nearest corner with the intention of dodging him, but immediately found herself in a ridiculous predicament. It was not a street at all, but a widish lane, ending abruptly after no more than fifty yards.

It was a nasty spot, a tipping place for garbage from the premises on either side, and as well, it was obvious, horse drawn vehicles parked there frequently. She had to retreat, and to her embarrassment, saw Parker standing at the opening end, watching her with some curiosity.

"Good morning, Mrs. Sandford," he said, gravely, raising his hat. "I called at your hotel, but you were absent."

She did not reply, and he added the rider that he hoped she was well.

There was no escape.

"Yes, thank you," she said. "I — I mistook my way."

"Very easily done in a strange town," he commented, his cool and unflickering gaze not revealing whether he believed her. "Mrs. Sandford, are the children with you?"

"No, they are at home. My husband had business here in Sandhurst, and I had some matters of my own which needed attention."

"Combining business and pleasure?" He fell into step alongside her, shortening his normally lengthy strides to match hers. There was no shaking him off. "I saw you at the play last night."

"And I saw you." Her anger rose against him, seeking any excuse to disturb his composure. "I found it most remarkable, Mr. Parker, that of all the people in the audience, you alone showed no emotion."

"I went with friends. Until I was in the theatre, I had no knowledge of the subject matter of the play. Otherwise I should not have gone. A friend of mine died during the Indian Mutiny in the most terrible circumstances. I can't amuse myself in that makebelieve."

"I was surprised to see that you were still in the country. I thought you were on your way back to New Zealand."

She overcame her reluctance to talk with him by telling herself that this was an opportunity to probe. His boldness in approaching her when he and her husband were avowed enemies disgusted and intrigued her at the same time.

"This is very likely my last visit to Australia, at least for some years," he rejoindered. "I'm travelling about inspecting sheep and draught horses, in order to improve our own stock."

"Why do you begrudge us our happiness, Mr. Parker?" She shot this at him with the intention of catching him off guard, and this time she was successful.

"What an extraordinary thing to say, Mrs. Sandford," he replied, after a thoughtful pause. "I think you owe me an explanation. For the life of me, I can't understand why my perfectly normal desire to see my nephew and niece upsets you so much."

"Is it necessary to explain, Mr. Parker? The lying campaign against my husband suggesting that he killed Mr. Tallence? And the strange discovery of Mr. Tallence's possessions out in the Whipstick, once again suggesting that Mr. Tallence has met with foul play?"

Then she stopped, colour rising in her face, as she realised just how far her tongue had bolted in her desire to protect the man she loved.

She saw the anger in his face, and was frightened.

"Mrs. Sandford," he said, in a voice which was little more than a hiss, "I advise you to forget what you've said, and equally, I advise you never, never to repeat such a thing to anyone. There is such a thing as slander, and if I hear another word of your ridiculous insinuations — one word, understand? — I'll not hesitate to have recourse to the law. Good day to you!"

Still making a pretence of courtesy, he touched his hat and left her, but such was his expression that she had no doubt that she was now included in the hatred he felt for Simon. She could not quite recall what Papa would have quoted on such an occasion, but she knew that he would have reprimanded her for letting the enemy know how much she knew.

Jane did not tell her husband about her encounter. She was ashamed of the way in which she had let her feelings run away with her, and afraid that she had made matters worse by confronting Parker with her suspicions.

When they returned to Curwood, three days later, she was astounded to learn, from Lily, that Mr. Parker, the children's maternal uncle, had called during their absence. Mr. Parker apparently showed a different side of his nature to Lily, for she described him as being ever such a nice gentleman, the kind Mr. and Mrs. MacBride used to entertain at their Sydney home in the old days before they went on that accursed trip to Britain. This was so obviously a poke at her own husband that Jane's hackles rose, and she was left wondering exactly what the venomous Mr. Parker had said to Lily.

"There's an old saying, Lily, 'Handsome is as handsome does'," she said, frigidly. "I dare say it could be changed to 'A gentleman is as a gentleman does'," and having delivered this rebuke for Lily to mull over and digest, she swept out to the enclosed portion of the veranda at the side of the house which now served as summer schoolroom.

Rodney was playing with the building blocks his father had brought him from Sandhurst. Dolly, hair tightly tied into two bunches, one on either side of her head, and white stockinged legs primly together under her short, pinafore-covered dress, sat at her table, earnestly forming her letters. Jane peremptorily beckoned to Chloris, and the governess arose and joined her outside.

"Miss McFarlane," she said, forgetting the friendly moments they had shared, "I believe Mr. James Parker called here during our absence?"

Chloris smiled, without guile, or so it seemed.

"Why, yes. He is my cousin, as you know, and the children's uncle. He was on his way back to Melbourne, to return to New Zealand, and he wished to say goodbye."

Goodbye. So, that coldmannered and mysterious man was definitely leaving the country. What a relief!

This was confirmed about ten days later when Simon received a letter from his sister Lucy, and in amongst the pages of chit-chat which that social-climbing matron considered of burning interest, was a brief paragraph to the effect that Caleb's brother had sailed for New Zealand. She could not understand why anyone should wish to settle among those ferocious Maoris with their endless wars, and put up with snowstorms in winter as well, but it was Mr. and Mrs. Parker's choice, and Jim's, too.

"I thought the Maoris were fighting in the North Island, not the South," murmured Sandford, smothering a smile as he finished reading his sister's outpourings aloud. "Still, Lucy has never been exactly enamoured of Jim, so very likely the wish was father to the thought."

Once again, Jane thought, what a relief! Now perhaps all that horrid business would fade away of its own accord.

She was wrong. The horrid business had scarcely begun.

11

SO determined was she to forget the allegations against her husband that Jane went to her bureau and opened the top right hand drawer wherein she had placed Hugh MacBride's sea-stained letter, for she intended to destroy it.

The letter had vanished. She searched through every drawer in the hope that she had had a lapse of memory, but when she failed to find it, she spoke to Lily. Had Lily seen the letter she had received from Mr. MacBride?

"Why, no, Miss Jane. 'Cept when you first read it, I haven't seen it at all."

Lily looked her straight in the face, with an almost forced innocence, or so Jane thought. The 'Miss Jane' was an added irritant, a sly sideways dig at Simon Sandford.

What a fool I was not to destroy it before going to Sandhurst, she told herself, later. Repulsive though the contents had been, the letter had been the only thing she had of Hugh MacBride's, and sentiment, rather than sense, had prompted her to keep it.

Neither had Sandford seen it after that first reading. He expressed surprise that his wife had kept the damned thing. His own impulse had been to toss the confounded letter into the kitchen fire.

Chloris — and James Parker. That was the explanation. Lily must have spread the word through the household that Mrs. Sandford had received a letter from beyond the grave, as it were, and Chloris had found it and handed it on to her scheming cousin. Jane remembered how angry Parker had been when she had accused him of spreading rumours about Simon, and how quickly he had countered with threats of an action for slander. Could it be that she had come too close to the truth for comfort, and that upon hearing about the letter, Parker had decided to destroy evidence which could link the rumours with himself?

She discussed her theory with Simon, and he mulled it over for some time. In the end, he told her not to carry the matter further. Perhaps Chloris was responsible for the letter vanishing, but then again, perhaps not. He was inclined to think that Lily had been the thief. She had been devoted to the MacBrides, and having sneaked a look at the letter, she must have realised just how discreditable it was to the memory of her late employer. On the other hand, he continued, with a smile, Jane had to admit that she had been extremely tired and upset before they had gone for their brief holiday at Sandhurst. It was possible that she had put the letter away in an odd corner and that it would reappear one day.

Eager though she was to tar James Parker with the brush of villainy, Jane had to admit that this could be so. She had been positive that she had put the letter in that particular drawer, but now she began to doubt her memory.

A few days after this, the young Irish housemaid came to Jane and told her that a young lad who called himself Tom Wells was at the back door and asking to see the mistress. She had the boy sent in to the small room she now used as a morning room, and was instantly struck by the way in which Tom Wells looked about himself in awestruck curiosity, and she realised that the lad had never before been in a house of any size.

"Yes, why did you wish to see me?"

He was not, she conceded to herself, a badlooking youth, although stringily built and terribly bashful.

"Mrs. Sandford," he blurted out, after some shifting from one foot to the other and looking in every direction but hers, "it's Ma. She's took real bad."

"Oh?" Jane was instantly sympathetic, but she remembered Mr. Wells' antagonism, and she was very cautious.

"I reckon she ought to have a doctor, but Pa won't have it and wouldn't let me go across to the township. Mrs. Sandford, she looks so awful. I'm scared she's done for."

"Has she been ill long?"

"Well, not ill 'zactly. There's bin another one on the way and somethin's gone wrong." Tom went bright red as he spoke of this taboo subject.

She saw the tears trembling behind the boy's lids and her heart melted. He was, after all, still a child, and it must have taken courage to go against his eccentric father's wishes and come here, to the hated squatter's home, to seek help for his mother.

"I know very little about such things," she said gently, "but there is someone here who may be able to help."

Lily must have had some experience in midwifery after years in Aunt Dorcas' service. When approached, Lily grumbled, and said from what she had heard, the Wells family were nothing more than trash.

"Mrs. Wells is a human being and a woman!" snapped Jane, and this rebuke had its effect.

This time, she drove. Practice was improving her skill and confidence with the reins. On the way, mindful of the way in which Simon had assumed that her mind had played her tricks over the matter of the missing letter, she decided to determine whether or not she had really seen a second man near the Wells mine. It was not pleasant to think that one was becoming victim to fancy.

"Your father and his partner must work very hard," she said, casually, over her shoulder, to Tom.

Tom gulped, as if scared.

"Pa ain't got no partner, Mrs. Sandford. He works the mine on his own, with a bit o' help from us kids."

It was a blow to Jane's self-esteem. After all that, the man must have been George, Tom's eldest brother, and the beard a trick of the light. George, caught stealing fruit, had had reason to dodge her.

As was to be expected, Joe Wells was obstreperous and stood in the women's way as they tried to enter the shack. Then, seeing Tom close behind, he began roaring in rage.

"Mr. Wells, if you so much as lay a finger on that boy, I'll have the law on you," said Jane, with a boldness she did not feel. Mr. Wells close up was an ugly customer. "Now, please stand aside so that we can attend to Mrs. Wells."

Mention of the law had an instant effect, and Jane surmised shrewdly that the miner had had trouble with the police at some time. Taking this as an advantage, she and Lily entered the shack.

It was not as bad as she had expected inside, being lined with whitewashed newspapers pasted against the walls of split timber which in turn had their chinks filled with clay. Unlike the pioneer Americans, who built their dwellings with the logs fitted horizontally, Australian bush settlers preferred to place the rough-hewn timber in a vertical position. Underfoot, the floor, surfaced with a mixture of clay and cow dung, was smooth, hard, and swept clean, undoubtedly by one of the little Wells girls, all of them nervous and plainly worried.

Originally, the shack had been divided into two rooms, a fairly large kitchen cum general living room, and sleeping quarters. The proliferation of the family had led to several flimsy additions, each reached through the last. Mrs. Wells, however, was in the original bedroom, on an iron bedstead, covered only by a sheet on this warm day.

This was something of a surprise. Jane had not expected the Wells family to be sufficiently well-off to afford such niceties as sheets, but then, the shack was furnished rather better than one would have anticipated, with store furniture instead of the makeshifts so common in the bush. Whatever was said locally, Wells was earning a living from his persistence in sticking here when everyone else had gone. Jane stopped feeling so sorry for them all, but her dislike of Mr. Wells increased in proportion. With his other faults, he was also a humbug.

Mrs. Wells was a tall, dark-haired woman in her early forties, weathered like all those of her sex unfortunate enough to live under harsh conditions. She must have possessed an Irish handsomeness once, and perhaps, in health, she was passable still. Now she had an intense, almost blue, whiteness in her face, and Lily immediately sent the little girl who sat at her mother's side out of the room.

"You need a doctor," said Lily bluntly, after a short conversation with Mrs. Wells.

"He'd never allow it. He doesn't like strangers comin' to the house."

"I'll do what I can," promised Lily. "First of all, let's put your feet up high."

204

Jane felt that she was not of much use here, and went outside, looking instinctively towards the mine entrance. For a moment, she saw him again, the man with the reddish beard. She had been right. There was someone else besides Mr. Wells working the mine. Now, this was a mystery. Why had Tom denied the existence of the other man?

She thought about it for a few moments, telling herself it was none of her business, but at the same time, she felt annoyed that her eyesight — and sanity — had been put at doubt. One of the little Wells girls came out to empty a bowl of water, and Jane asked her whom the man who worked with her father might be.

"Oh, that's Uncle Jack," said the child carelessly, but almost straight away, her small hand flew up to cover her mouth, and she stared up at Jane in dismay. "I shouldn't't've told you," she whispered, frightened.

Then she turned and bolted indoors.

"Well, she's lost the baby," said Lily on their way back to Curwood, "but with all those other children, you can't help wondering if it's not a blessing. I'd like to have a while alone with that husband of hers. Too mean to send for the doctor! They're not as short as you'd think. A very funny state of affairs there, if you ask me."

To this last, Jane silently agreed. She decided not to mention 'Uncle Jack', not wishing to bring punishment down on Tom and the little girl.

"I'll go again tomorrow, if it's all right with you," continued Lily. "I can't do much beyond make sure she's comfortable and no worse, but just having another grown woman there to talk to made her feel better."

"Yes, you may." But she was not altogether happy with the idea. "Do be careful, Lily. Mr. Wells is a very peculiar man."

"Don't worry. I won't poke into what doesn't concern me," replied Lily. "Not with that Wells brute ready to pull visitors apart."

A development the next day put the Wells family and their mystery out of Jane's mind for the time being.

It was, she noted, as she made an entry

in her daily journal, the third of March. Summer was almost over, according to the calendar, but the days continued hot and muggy, demanding the relief of a thunderstorm to ease the unceasing sultriness.

A year ago, Jane reflected, pausing and stroking under her chin with the top of her pen, Papa had still been alive, and so excited about the letter he had received from the solicitor representing old Horatio Wilson's interests in Britain. What a wretched, windy, wet day that had been, and how grey and dismal the narrow back streets. Her shoes had been almost worn out, and her feet were soaking when she came in from their poor little shopping.

Papa, despite the cough which had lingered on through winter, had been jubilant. He had been eagerly awaiting her return, and at first scarcely noticed her drenched state. There would be nothing to worry about, he said. Soon, she would be acknowledged as joint heiress to the old man's fortune, and their troubles would be at an end. Belatedly, he saw that she was wet and chilled.

"Take off your wet things, Jenny," he insisted, bustling about in his joy, "and warm yourself before our fire. See, I've used most of our coal! We deserve a little celebration! Ah, my dear, truly it was said that the meek shall inherit the earth."

"Papa," she had said, tense and shivering, "we'll have to postpone our celebration. I saw him in the High Street. I don't think that he saw me, but Evan Whiteside is here!"

Papa's cheerfulness had instantly vanished, and he had become wary and alert.

"We must go then, Jenny," he had said. "How ridiculous it all is. You, my daughter, are about to become a rich woman, and we still have to creep out of our lodgings like rats on the run."

That had been the beginning of the journey which had brought her here to Curwood, a journey of peril, tragedy and intense joy.

On that later third of March, Dolly went out to play after her lessons were finished, running about the large garden with her young brother, for she was forbidden to go beyond the gate without an adult. Simon Sandford, who had been at Omega for three days, returned during the afternoon, hot, tired and exasperated, for as he told his wife, nothing had gone right. A well which had been sunk had yielded only brackish water, there had been a small grass fire which, although soon brought under control, had caused great disruption, and to crown everything, it had been found that some of the sheep were diseased.

Whilst he was recounting this saga of disaster, Dolly came in, followed by her little brother. She was carrying her favourite doll, a flaxen-haired beauty with staring blue eyes, improbably red cheeks and a slightly battered nose.

"Papa," she asked, "do you like Christabel's new necklace?"

About Christabel's neck was looped a thin gold chain with small red stones set at intervals, with a larger stone set in a frame of twisted gold. The stones were garnets, and although the trinket could not be counted as being of great value, it was still far too expensive a bauble to be a child's plaything.

"Dolly, where did you find that?"

demanded her governess, who had been invited to take tea with Mr. and Mrs. Sandford.

"I found it," said Dolly levelly. "It was on the bench under the big tree."

The big tree was an old gum which had somehow survived the clearing, and had remained as the only large tree near the homestead. While this exchange was going on, Sandford was staring at the necklace as if unable to believe his eyes.

"Are you sure, Dolly?" he broke in, and the little girl nodded demurely.

"It was on the bench," she repeated, and her brother joined in anxiously to confirm that what his sister had said was true.

"Give me Christabel."

He took the doll from the child, and carefully unfastened the necklace, holding it up for inspection.

"Dolly, you must have known that this was not meant for your doll," he said, and there was something so strained about his voice that Jane, who until now had been more puzzled than concerned, knew that something was wrong.

"But it was for me, Papa," protested

Dolly, and then she took from the pocket of her pinafore a scrap of paper with one word, her name, printed on it in large block letters. "This was on the bench, and the necklace was on top of it."

"Dolly, someone must have given it to you. Whom?" There was a desperation in her father's tone, and he turned to Chloris, anger darkening his goodlooking face. "Miss McFarlane, your common sense should have told you that this trinket was not meant for a child."

"Mr. Sandford," said Chloris, calmly, "until the past five minutes, I had never before in my entire life seen that necklace."

Chloris's demeanour was unexcited, but there was in her words an inflexion which indicated that she meant to stand her ground and that she had no intention of accepting an accusation.

"I wish to talk to Mrs. Sandford alone," said Simon after a moment's reflection. "And I'll keep the necklace for the time being," he added, and Dolly burst into tears.

"It's mine," she wailed as Chloris firmly propelled her from the room in the company of her brother.

"Someone," said the man, grimly, as he closed the door after them, "is playing a joke. A grotesque joke, Jane. That necklace belonged to Sarah. I gave it to her on our first wedding anniversary, and from the time she ran away from our home until this day, I've never seen it again."

"Simon!" she exclaimed, coming close to him, and taking the necklace from him and holding it up to the light. "Are you sure? This is a fairly common design."

"Of course I'm sure. Look closely at the work about the largest stone. Intertwined 's's'. We had the same initials, you see."

She had to use her imagination, but the twists did resemble the letter 's'.

"But who on earth . . . "

"That's it. Who on earth!" He was very angry and upset. "Miss Chloris McFarlane. Everything points to her. Jim Parker put her up to it. Well, that's the end. She's going back to Melbourne immediately. What she hopes to gain from this kind of behaviour I can't imagine, but I will not tolerate it.

Jim visiting here behind our backs was enough, but this is the last straw."

Jane was dubious.

"I don't think she was lying when she told us that she'd never seen the necklace before, and surely Mr. Parker would not be . . . so obvious."

She felt a little guilty herself, because she had not told Simon about her encounter with Parker that morning in Sandhurst.

"Are you sure that the necklace wasn't amongst your own possessions?" she probed, and he turned on her so angrily that she was startled.

"What are you suggesting? That I suffered from some sort of brainstorm and put the necklace on the bench myself? Jane, don't be ridiculous. I've had no reason to treasure Sarah's trinkets. No, she took her jewellery with her when she left."

An idea took hold in Jane's mind, but she decided that this was not the moment to mention it. Later, when Simon was in a better mood, she would place it before him. There was someone else who could have had the necklace, Sarah's lover, supposedly in California.

"I'm going to ask everyone on this run — and I mean everyone — until I find the culprit," concluded Sandford, and in a final gesture of anger, he flung it down on to the table amidst the cups and saucers.

Jane sought out Chloris, not caring for the task, and questioned the governess again, but the other young woman steadfastly denied that she knew anything about the necklace's strange reappearance. In fact, Chloris took such offence that she offered to leave the next day, and Jane found herself in the difficult and rather humiliating position of having to ask her to reconsider.

"I'm very fond of my cousin Jim," said Chloris in the end, only partly mollified, "but I would never help him to play such a cruel and pointless practical joke. As far as that goes, I cannot imagine Jim stooping to such a thing. He has no liking for Mr. Sandford, but I assure you, Mrs. Sandford, he has no wish to distress you by reminding you of a former chapter in your husband's life. And poor little Dolly is very upset, and can't understand what all the fuss is about."

An angry Simon Sandford was not so easily soothed. He was going to write to Lucy and demand that she find another governess immediately. If that other woman was not yet well enough to come, that was too bad. They should never have inconvenienced themselves on her behalf.

Jane pointed out the difficulties she would face if she had to add the supervision of the children to her many other duties. He was away at Omega so often nowadays that she was, in fact, almost managing Curwood on her own.

After some more grumbling, he agreed to give Chloris the benefit of the doubt. However, Miss McFarlane must have thought it over during the night, because the next day she announced that she would leave almost straight away, when Billy Harden set out on his return journey after his weekly delivery.

Chloris was evidently one of those outwardly placid persons whose wrath sets hard with the passing of time. She told Jane frankly that she had put herself out to come to Curwood at a time when she would much have preferred to have been in Melbourne near her fiancé. She had accepted this temporary post out of sympathy for her little Sandford relatives, but Mr. Sandford's wild and extraordinary accusations were more than she could tolerate. From Jane, she begged understanding, and added an assurance that she did not blame Mrs. Sandford for what had happened. She was sorry to leave Mrs. Sandford in the lurch, but she could not tolerate aspersions upon her good name.

Dolly wept uncontrollably as Chloris left with Billy Harden. She refused comfort from her stepmother, but instead rushed to the accommodating arms of Lily.

"Mr. Sandford should've known better," grumbled Lily later. "All this chopping and changing isn't good for children. As for what's going on in this house — letters disappearing and necklaces appearing — I'll be leaving myself if there's much more of it."

12

MARCH dragged on, hot and unremittingly dry. Even the trees now had a dusty, greyish look about them. The ponds which had been dug for the stock — dams as they are called in Australia — were less than half full of muddy water, and an anxious scanning of the sky became a daily habit.

The ones least affected by this prolonged summer were Dolly and Rodney. Jane set lessons daily for Dolly, but with the demands of the household upon her, she could not devote as much time to the children as had Chloris McFarlane, and they were both quick to take advantage of this, spending the days in unaccustomed and blissful freedom.

Looking back in later years, when she was happily settled in another place, Jane could realise that during the time following Chloris's departure, she deliberately busied herself with all manner of tasks, some of which should have been left to the servants. She had to do this to keep her mind from brooding over the unsolved enigmas of the vanishing letter and the even stranger arrival of the necklace. Simon still averred that Miss McFarlane had been the culprit in both cases. She had feigned indignation, he said, in a clumsy attempt to divert suspicion from herself. Now that she had gone, he continued, there would be an end to the mischief.

He was wrong, as it turned out. Dramatically, the whole picture changed, and a new and frightening dimension at once solved and deepened the mystery.

Simon rode off to Omega, very early in the day, promising to return before the end of the week. Jane could not pretend to like his absences, but she understood that it was necessary to him that he should have his own holding. On this particular morning, she set Dolly her lessons, saw to it that Rodney was sufficiently occupied, and then retreated to her correspondence.

The letter had come from her Melbourne solicitor the previous day, and she had

218

not yet shown it to Simon. She was, said the legal gentleman, spending far too much money on Curwood. Furniture? Household utensils? Repairs? How on earth did the trustees of her grandfather's estate think she should live? In an almost empty house?

Jane decided to answer this letter without any further ado, and point out that the greater part of this expenditure was absolutely necessary, and not likely to be repeated in the near future. She had done little more than write the date at the top of the paper when there was an interruption.

One of the station hands had come over to the homestead in a great hurry. He had found Bevis, he said, on the river bank, nibbling at a bit of grass which had somehow survived the long dry spell. Of Mr. Sandford, there was no sign, and it seemed probable that either Mr. Sandford had dismounted on his way to Omega and Bevis had wandered off, or Mr. Sandford had been thrown.

As if listening to an echo, Jane heard her own voice calmly ordering an immediate search with every man available taking part. If there had been an accident, it must have occurred somewhere along the track to Omega, and if the horse had returned in a comparatively short time, not so very far from the Curwood homestead. Then, she ordered the little spring-cart to be harnessed immediately, and still in the calm, detached fashion, she told Lily to pack a basket with the items needed if Mr. Sandford had been injured.

All the while, this efficient, cool-headed Jane was issuing orders, Inside of her, there was another terrified, weeping person, begging God not to complete her triumvirate of tragedy by making her a widow after a scant three months of marriage. Despite Lily's protests, at the last Jane left her behind to keep an eye on the children. The thought was in the back of her head that Dolly and Rodney liked and trusted Lily. If the worst had happened, Lily could be relied upon to care for the children.

Accompanied by the three men who had been at the home station on that hot morning, Jane followed the track to Omega, crossing at the ford where a bare inch of water trickled over a rocky floor, and then up the incline to a cleft in the low line of hills with their grey outcrops of rock jutting against the brown sameness of summer's end. Beyond the cleft, the country rolled away in the same pattern, mile after mile, until it rose into the distant blue ranges which divided this land from the coastal plains to the south. Once, she saw a great eagle poised above a hilltop, balancing on an updraught of air, motionless for seconds, and then dropping like lead in a shot tower to a chosen prey below. Further along, a number of crows wheeled in a half circle, as if inspecting carrion on the ground, but, thankfully, they flew to a large tree and roosted in its branches.

How absurd it was that she should think that Simon was dead. He was a strong man, in the early prime of his life, with many years of healthy, vigorous existence before him. Just as she was about to give way to her most desperate thoughts, she saw him, walking towards them, dishevelled and dusty, but obviously unhurt.

"I'm certainly glad to see you — and

the cart," he said, cheerfully, as they all met.

"Simon, what happened?"

He stood quite still, taking deep breaths, fanning himself with his wide-brimmed hat. Mindful that he must be thirsty, she took the water bottle from the basket and handed it to him. He smiled, rather crookedly.

"I see that you came prepared for the worst," he said, and with a shrug, added: "Bevis threw me. A snake crossed the track and the brute reared. I was lucky. I landed in a patch of scrub which broke my fall before I rolled down the slope. I'm filthy, but that's better than being hurt."

What a relief it was, and as he climbed up into the cart, he gave her hand a quick, light squeeze.

His easy explanation of the incident was a lie, as he confessed later in their bedroom, as he changed from his dusty clothes. The truth about his accident was that someone had fired a shot at him.

"Simon!" She was completely aghast. "Hadn't we best send a message to the police?"

222

"Waste of time. The scoundrel must be miles away by now." There was a false joviality in his voice which alerted her.

"What are you keeping from me?"

He was silent, with an uncertainty in his expression.

"Was it Joe Wells?" She uttered the first name which came into her head so as to avoid mentioning the one belonging to the man she suspected. At the same time, the idea of James Parker coldly and calmly awaiting Simon Sandford could not be digested unless one brought in an unpleasant corollary. Someone must have told him when Simon would be leaving Curwood. One of the men? Or, Lily?

"Joe Wells? Why should he? I'd like to see the end of that tribe, but I haven't had any direct dealings with him. No, I hardly like mentioning this, Jane, in case I'm wrong. But I'm sure that I knew the voice. He called out to me. 'Sandford!' Just the one word. I was so surprised that I reined in Bevis. Then he fired just one shot. I felt the wind as it passed my head. I don't know whether it was done to scare me, or whether he missed."

"It *was* James Parker." She said it flatly, almost accusingly. The strange thing was that she did not really want to believe it. It was too far-fetched, too fantastic, that Parker should carry on this crazy vendetta against the man who had married his adored twin sister. Even more fantastic was the notion that Parker could have drawn Chloris, and perhaps Lily, into his conspiracy.

"No. It wasn't Jim. I didn't see him, but the voice — I'm sure about the voice. He had a strange way of saying Sandford, almost as if it were two words. I think it was Jack Tallence."

Jane could hear the children playing in the garden below. Idly, she thought, I should go down and set Dolly to doing her lessons. She is running quite wild these last days. Then emotion broke, and she flung herself against Simon, her arms about him, her cheek pressing against his chest.

"Oh, no!" she wept. "Simon, you must go to the police. We can't handle this alone. Inspector Burke, your friend, must be back from his holiday by now. You can send word to him. Tell him that Jack

Tallence is tormenting you in every way he is able."

He tipped up her chin, and then kissed her, hard, on the mouth.

"You are," he said, slowly, "the most remarkable little lady. It's as if you can enter my head. If I went to our local sergeant in the township, or even to the officer in charge at Sandhurst, they'd act as if I were deluded. They would not credit that my dead wife's lover is carrying on a vendetta against me. It should be the other way about, they'd say. But I believe that Tallence blamed me for Sarah's death. After all, it was Rodney's birth which killed her, if you overlook the way in which she bolted off to the wilds in the middle of winter. But I'll write to Burke. He has enough influence and reputation to stir up some interest amongst the local force."

"But it could take *weeks*, Simon." She raised her tearstained face to his. "I'm so frightened that he's no longer content with teasing you. He's a madman, and he's out there, somewhere, hiding, waiting for you. And, there must be someone here, perhaps in this house, or out in the men's quarters, telling him what is happening."

"She's gone," said her husband. "Now it's all guesswork on his part."

Jane disengaged herself from his embrace, and walked slowly to the tall, rectangular window which overlooked the garden and the picket gate. The children were quiet now. Dolly sat on the bench where the necklace had been left, and played with Christabel. Rodney dogged the Chinese gardener, offering advice which the Celestial could have hardly understood, although with his race's characteristic fondness for children, he patiently allowed the small boy to 'help' him.

"I can't believe that Chloris would be a party to an attempted murder," she stated.

"I doubt whether Chloris, or even Jim, expected things to go so far. They probably only intended to make a fool of me. Jim's back in New Zealand, and Chloris is back in Melbourne, no doubt telling all and sundry her own version of why she left so suddenly. I'm convinced it's Tallence on his own,

226

now. I can't believe that he meant to kill me this morning. Now I've had time to recover myself, I'm sure our meeting was accidental and that he gave way to an impulse. I wouldn't be surprised if he gave himself a bigger scare than I had when I fell off Bevis. He must have thought he'd killed me! He could well be halfway to Melbourne by now, hoping to find a ship that'll be cleared out of port before my body is found."

Then, apparently seeing by her alarmed expression that she was far from reassured, he smiled gently.

"Now, dearest, trust me to handle things in my own way. And I think it is time for our lunch. My long walk made me very hungry."

While Simon had made it clear that she must leave everything to him, Jane made her own plans. Again and again her mind returned to that mysterious Uncle Jack who bolted out of sight whenever anyone visited the Wells shack. Later, she spoke to Lily, not about Mr. Sandford's misfortune that morning, but about Mrs. Wells. Had Mrs. Wells fully recovered? What with the upset of Miss McFarlane leaving so unexpectedly, she had not had time to enquire.

"I saw the lad, Tom, this morning," said Lily, rather cautiously, as if knowing quite well that Mrs. Sandford had something on her mind besides Mrs. Wells' health. "He told me that his mother is up and about."

"Tom? Where did you see him?" Jane's voice betrayed her astonishment, and Lily paused before replying, as if considering carefully.

"Why, right out there between our garden fence and the men's quarters, Mrs. Sandford. I saw him walking past, so I ran out and asked him about his mother."

"Lily, what was Tom doing here?"

Jane felt as if she were looking into a toy kaleidoscope. Patterns kept forming, and moving, and changing. If only one could make a pattern hold, and set firmly into place. But young Tom Wells had moved into the pattern, and his segment fitted so perfectly into what had been forming in her imagination that her heart pounded with excitement.

Lily was looking a little sheepish.

"He's over here from time to time," she replied, almost offhandedly. "There's no harm in it, but I know Mr. Sandford would be annoyed, so I don't mention it, and neither does anyone else. I don't mean to offend you, Mrs. Sandford, but Mr. Sandford keeps a tight check on everything. Tom comes over to see the blacksmith. He brings over little things which need fixing at the forge. Oh, he pays in kind, working the bellows and stoking up the fire, and if he wants a few nails, he brings his own rods. Old Bart doesn't mind. Mr. Wheeler used to allow it, they say, because Mrs. Wells did his mending for him."

This was a revelation to Jane, and brought home sharply just how easy it was for all kinds of activities to be taking place right under employers' noses without them being aware of any of it.

Young Tom Wells, for whom she had a soft spot, and thought of as being much nicer than his bumptious brother George, could easily be the person who had left the necklace, and perhaps the one who had crept into the house and removed the letter after getting wind of it from servants' gossip.

Uncle Jack had to be Jack Tallence. It fitted so perfectly now that one had found the missing factor. Even the unexpectedly good furniture in the Wells shack made sense, for it could have been purchased with bribe money paid by Tallence. At the same time, it explained why Chloris had been so blind that day. She naturally would not have admitted to having seen Jack Tallence.

Jane's mind was made up. She was going to get to the bottom of the whole stupid affair once and for all, and the best way, she was convinced, was by having a stern talk with Mrs. Wells. To do this, she needed to take Lily into her confidence.

"Shot at Mr. Sandford!"

Lily's mouth dropped open, and her round, plain face showed her partial disbelief.

"If that's true, Mrs. Sandford," she continued, quickly recovering herself, "it's a matter for policemen, not women like us."

"But don't you see, Lily, there's no

230

real proof. We have to talk with Mrs. Wells and point out just how deeply into trouble she could find herself if that man really is Jack Tallence."

"H'm. I don't like it one bit, but I can see you're not going to be satisfied until you've done what your mind is set on doing."

One result of Simon's unfortunate experience was that he decided against going to Omega that week. Instead, he busied himself nearer to home, and judging by certain sullen mutterings, it was not a popular move. Mr. Wheeler, Jane heard from Lily, in spite of his obstreperous attitude towards women, had been well liked by the Curwood men, mainly because he scorned domestic niceties, and turned a generally blind eye towards any carousing which took place in the men's quarters. As long as the sheep kept in health and the required number of bales went off annually to the wool sales, he was tolerant to the point of laziness.

"Have you thought," said Lily, almost idly, "that one of the men might have fired the shot at Mr. Sandford?"

They were on their way, taking

advantage of Simon's absence checking the amount of feed left for the animals a mile or so north of Curwood. Lily hated the whole enterprise, but Jane was determined. Mrs. Wells did not conceal her astonishment when they arrived, but after some hesitation and much wiping of her hands on her grubby apron, she offered tea.

As she spoke, she idly waved a leafy twig to and fro to discourage the flies which came through the open door. Considering everything, the shack was well kept, but outside there was plenty of encouragement for that universal Australian pest, the fly. Fowls, goats, cows, the ancient horse which worked the puddling machine, all contributed rich breeding grounds, augmented by the noisome pool below the mine which doubled as rubbish tip.

Jane exchanged a quick glance with Lily, and politely thanked Mrs. Wells for her kind thought, but today she had little time to spare. First of all, she wished to know whether Mrs. Wells' health had improved.

By now, the miner's wife was becoming

suspicious. She knew quite well that the Mrs. Sandfords of this world did not normally call socially upon the likes of herself. Jane wasted no further time in coming to the point.

"Mrs. Wells," she said, bluntly, "you must be honest with us. We both know that there is another adult man besides your husband living here, and that for some reason he hides from visitors. Is that man Jack Tallence?"

While Jane was speaking, Mrs. Wells' greenish eyes became almost glazed, as if concealing some rapid and intense mental process.

"What man?" she mumbled.

"Mrs. Wells, one of your little girls called him 'Uncle Jack' within my hearing. A man named Jack Tallence fired a shot at my husband two days ago. Please, Mrs. Wells, do remember that you have nine children and that most of them are still very young. If you and Mr. Wells are charged with harbouring, you could both go to prison. If that happened, who would look after your children?"

Mrs. Wells had gone deathly pale, almost as much so as when she had been ill, and her big, work-worn hands arose to press against her temples.

"Holy Mother of Jesus," she muttered. "I shouldn't have agreed to it, never!" Her expression had become subtly cunning. "All right," she continued, recovering herself. "I don't know what you're talking about. Till you said his name, so help me, I'd never heard of this Tallence cove in all me life."

"What shouldn't you have agreed to?" insisted Jane.

There was a long silence, broken when a couple of the smaller Wells children appeared in the doorway, only to be shooed away by their mother. This interruption must have served to make up Mrs. Wells' mind, because now she replied to Jane's question.

"Mrs. Sandford, what's it to you? He's me brother, and what was a body to do? He's me blood, me only kin in this country."

"Jack Tallence?"

This was an unexpected twist. Sarah Sandford, whatever her shortcomings, had been raised as a young lady. To imagine her throwing her bonnet over

234

the windmill for Mrs. Wells' brother was difficult.

"I tell you, Mrs. Sandford, I dunno anyone called Tallence. Now leave us alone."

"All right. I'll send word to the police that you are hiding a man here. The man Tallence had been engaging in a stupid vendetta against my husband, and I want him brought to justice."

Mrs. Wells burst into tears.

"Mrs. Sandford, I thought you was a real kind lady. Why are you doing this to me? Jack's been a bit foolish, I'll own, but he's hurt no one since he's been here. All he wants is to live out his last days in peace, him sufferin' from the consumption like he is."

"All I want to know is whether your brother is Jack Tallence," persisted the determined Jane.

Mrs. Wells blew her nose on a corner of her apron, and glared defiantly at her inquisitor.

"No, and why should he call hisself that? He's an Irishman, through and through, and proud o' bein' O'Shea. All right, Mrs. High and Mighty Sandford, go and tell the police Dancing Jack O'Shea's here, but he'll be fifty miles away and no tracks behind him afore they come."

The tears had stopped as quickly as they had started, and Mrs. Wells lost all patience, for now she thumped her fist on the table.

"Now get out of me 'ouse," she yelled, "and don't come back."

An apology had to be in order.

"Mrs. Wells, I'm sorry, but . . . "

"Get out! Both of ye! Comin' here with your trumped up stories! What would Jack shoot at that husband of yourn for? Tell me that! Dancing Jack the Gentleman Bushranger they called 'im. Never fired a shot in anger in his life!"

Lily had taken hold of Jane's arm, and she tugged it, hard.

"Mrs. Sandford," she urged, "do come along. Let's get ourselves out of here."

Driving back to Curwood, handling the reins with her newly found competence, Jane had to admit that she had made a complete fool of herself. The only compensation was that she now knew that the man she had seen had been no figment of a disordered mind.

Lily was able to tell her something about Dancing Jack O'Shea. He was reputed to have been one of the robbers who had accomplished a great criminal coup of the gold rush. Several years earlier, a party of daring thieves had rowed out to a ship, laden with gold, which lay at anchor off Melbourne. They had overcome the few crew members on board, removed the enormous quantity of gold, and had vanished, it seemed, into thin air.

None of the treasure had been recovered, and no arrests made. Some time later, O'Shea had been arrested in a brothel after one of the girls had passed on to police that she believed their free-spending client was the notorious bushranger, Dancing Jack O'Shea had been convicted on several counts of robbery under arms, and sent to prison. Lily deduced that he must have escaped during her absence from the country, and she advised her mistress to send word to the nearest police station immediately.

"But if he is dying of consumption — oh, I wish I'd left well alone," responded Jane, rather wretchedly.

Everything had fitted so well, the name Jack, the man's peculiar behaviour, and Tom's frequent, unnoticed, visits to Curwood, but all Jane had now to show for the morning's work was a sharp object lesson in the dangers of jumping to conclusions.

Lily laughed, shortly.

"I don't doubt," she said, "that Mrs. Wells told you that tale to make her sorry for her rascally brother."

The other did not reply. The horse trotted on apathetically in the heat, and its driver made no effort to hasten the beast. Despite her calm face beneath its protective brim, Jane was inwardly in a turmoil of doubt and conflict.

She had turned the Wells family into bitter enemies, and for what purpose? Papa had warned her once that imagination, like fire, was a good servant but a poor master. Holy Writ backed his admonishment, necessary in a life requiring frequent and realistic summings-up of difficult situations.

"'Let them perish through their own imaginations'," he had quoted.

Certainly, although imagination was Papa's constant tool, he had used it with skill and with an eye to profit.

"It's our duty," continued Lily lugubriously, "to let the authorities know about Jack O'Shea."

"Oh, he's probably gone by now."

It was more than a statement. It was a wish.

13

JANE SANDFORD was mistress of Curwood, an heiress, a happily married woman, and in every way a person with a vested interest in respectability. Unfortunately, she was also Papa's daughter, firmly instructed to forget the past and step bravely into the new life he had arranged for her. Only the past, and those many months of a footloose, hunted existence, refused to be forgotten.

Common sense told her that Jack O'Shea was a thoroughly bad lot who deserved to be returned to his prison cell, but at the same time, in spite of Lily's cynicism, she believed Mrs. Wells' story that her brother was ill. It was not so much that O'Shea's wicked career could be justified, but the rush of fellow feeling for his unlucky sister which made Jane waver on the side of keeping his secret.

The reins were limp in her hands, and glad of a respite, the horse paused and put his head down to nibble at a few dry stalks of grass which had survived in the scant shade of a lanky tree which had scattered its peeled bark across the firmly packed dirt.

It was as if she were transported back in time to that cool day in Bristol, when she had been choosing books and had glanced up to see Evan Whiteside. He had paid for the books, she remembered vividly, and not for the first time, wondered whether he had taken them back for a refund. Probably. He could hardly be well off on a policeman's pay.

"Is something wrong, Mrs. Sandford? Are you feeling unwell?"

Lily's concerned voice broke into her black little reverie, and Jane shook her head, trying to wrest herself from the haunting past.

"No. The heat worries me, though, and I wish we would have a cool change. The hot weather has gone on and on."

"There'll be a big storm before it changes," said Lily, gloomily. It was as if she were determined to look on the darker side. "I can feel it building up."

The rest of the short journey was

completed in silence. For the rest of the day, Jane found herself falling into abstraction, for Jack O'Shea's precarious state of freedom had reminded her, all too bitterly, that it would be many years before she could safely contemplate a trip Home to England. Jenny Turner, of umpteen changing addresses, had been absorbed into Jane Sandford, of Curwood, Victoria, Australia, and she had been so worried lately about Simon that her sad and harried past had become insignificant.

Should she have confessed all to Simon? During their brief engagement, she had feared that he would have demanded his freedom if he had known the truth. After marriage, which had been so blissful in spite of recent worries, she made up her mind that silence was the best policy.

Yet, obversely, it would have been the greatest relief to confide about Papa. She was not by nature a hypocrite, but Papa had been so insistent that she must follow his instructions carefully, and because he was dying, she had sworn to do so, knowing that it gave him peace to know that his only child would be safe and affluent.

Papa really had been a clergyman once. She was not sure why he had been defrocked, but she knew that he had taken the death of her mother very hard. For a while, she suspected, he had taken to drinking very heavily, and this had led to his disgrace and expulsion from the church.

He had a minor gift for writing, and with a small income from his own family — a species of bribe to keep him out of their way — he managed to keep them both, though in frugal circumstances. Eventually, he had sent her away to school, and during the holidays she spent with him, he seemed to be, although certainly not rich, fairly comfortable. Inevitably, the time came when it was no longer possible to keep her at school. She was a young woman past eighteen, and it was soon after she had joined him that a first inkling of the truth was revealed.

Papa did write little pieces for the magazines, and even sometimes for religious periodicals, but the remuneration from these efforts was minuscule. The income from his family had petered out, why she never learned, and his main source of money was through cunningly composed begging letters to carefully selected marks.

During the time she had been with Papa, he had been Major Paul Tinsdale, one-legged survivor of Waterloo, reduced to the direst possible straits, Captain Peter Tracy who had spent months on an island in the Pacific where the heathen begged for The Word, and his best creation, Pensley Turner, distraught father whose daughter had been captured by Arab pirates.

The more hardheaded the business magnate, the more likely he was to fall for these fabrications, observed Papa, smiling gently as he sorted out the latest batch of letters containing donations to the cause.

Yet, all through this, Papa did not fail to recognise his own obligations. He kept only what was required to balance their own modest budget. The rest he used to assist the needy. In his rusty old clerical garb, he had frequently been the recipient of tearful thanks from despairing widows and the aged who lived in terror of the workhouse. The ragged schools received a substantial anonymous donation every few months to assist with the education of pauper children, but it was the plight of soldiers' wives which aroused Papa to his most inspired efforts — and led to his downfall.

"Left to fend for themselves whilst their menfolk go off to rib their lives in a stupid war to bolster up the Turks! And all instigated by that upstart Bonaparte!" fumed Papa, after watching soldiers march through the streets on their way to embark for the Crimea.

This moment saw the birth of Pensley Turner, defrauder of the pompous great and benefactor of many a poor woman whose crime was that she had married a common soldier. Only a proportion of the wives were able to accompany their men to the theatre of war, and wretched though their lot might be, at least they could rely upon some sustenance. leaving the others to rely upon their own resources was a national scandal, declared Papa. (The iron-willed Miss Florence

Nightingale unknowingly concurred with this, and used her excellent connections to ensure, eventually, that a system of allotments from a soldier's pay would help provide for his family.)

In the meantime, Pensley Turner did his best, until he over-reached himself. What Papa wrote in that fatal letter to a Very Important Great Man, Jane never discovered, but the reward was beyond the author's wildest hopes. Two thousand pounds.

The bank draft was cashed without delay, and when Papa had taken out his own small commission, he had sent the rest directly to a public fund for the succour of Crimean widows and their children. With the war just ended, their needs were more urgent than those of the survivors' wives.

Unfortunately, the Very Important Great Man had been in a state of euphoria following a grand banquet when he had sent off that bank draft. A few days later, his secretary had brought the matter to his notice, and the fat was in the fire! The police were called, and the address on Pensley Turner's letter visited.

The culprit and his daughter had already left, but their trail was not hard to follow. Papa, with his prematurely silvered locks, was a distinctive figure, and there was nothing for it but to retreat to Ostend. The episode at Bristol had been almost a case of history repeated, for Evan Whiteside had cornered Jane minutes before their boat was due to leave for the Channel crossing. He was only weeks out of the army, and eager to make up for time lost in his usual occupation of policeman. Unfortunately for him, Whiteside was inclined to put on airs, and his gentlemanly behaviour in handing Jane into a hansom for transport to the police station gave her the chance to jump out of the other side and bolt.

As periods of the past extending over a considerable length of time do when viewed in retrospect, all this chased through Jane's mind in a few minutes. Although she found it hard to shake off that sympathy for the reprobate Jack O'Shea, another view of those adventures she had shared with Papa began to take shape.

Papa had always made it seem such

fun, and during the harried months they had been together, he had appeared to be a sort of latter day Robin Hood in the unlikely guise of a frail, silverhaired, middle-aged man. Unfortunately, from her present situation, the whole affair was starting to assume a slightly tarnished aspect.

Resolutely, Jane thrust aside this disloyalty. She owed everything to Papa, including her wonderful marriage. As for Evan Whiteside — no wonder that in her dreams he appeared in association with an owl. How silly it was to persist in fearing that blundering man who had been so easily tricked on two occasions!

Immediately pressing was the problem of what to tell Simon about her morning's work. All along, he had made it plain that it was his prerogative to cope with the elusive Jack Tallence. She told Lily not to mention to anyone what had transpired.

"Well, everyone round the place knows we've been *somewhere*," grumbled Lily, plainly puzzled at Jane's reluctance to bring O'Shea to justice.

"I'll tell Mr. Sandford myself," Jane assured her.

As she had anticipated, he was annoyed.

"If you had these notions about Mrs. Wells' brother, why didn't you tell me? Good heavens, girl, haven't you any idea of how dangerous some of these men are? I hope you've learnt a lesson and won't go off on any more expeditions without proper protection."

"Oh, Simon, I'm sorry." She was brushing out her hair before her dressing table as she spoke, and now she put down the brush and began plaiting her hair preparatory to retiring for the night. "I know I let my imagination run away with me, but I thought I'd found where Tallence was hiding, and I wanted so to help you."

"Jane, dearest, you don't have to perform silly deeds of derring-do to prove that you love me."

In the mirror, his reflection was so handsome that her heart turned over. The lamplight softened the small imperfections, the little lines and the settling of features natural to a man in his thirties, leaving her to wonder that such an attractive man should care for her.

"Please," he continued, "never do such a thing again! I'm quite alarmed to think of what you've been doing behind my back now that you've learnt to handle the reins."

"This morning was the first time," she said, glowing a little inside because he worried about her. "With the children to watch over, my days have been very full, though when the weather cools, I do intend taking them out on a few short excursions."

He placed his strong hands on her shoulders, his fingertips pressing gently into her flesh so that she felt excitement rising within her.

"Jane, this isn't the peaceful, law abiding countryside of England. There are a lot of little shacks left by the miners in isolated spots, right through these goldfield areas. Most of them are tumbling down, but any one of them could be sheltering a villain. I know your Lily is formidable, but two women are no match for an armed man." He smiled. "In a way, what you did today was for the best. At least, one scoundrel has been frightened away, because I'm sure Mr. O'Shea packed and left hours ago, and every trace of his having been there with him."

"But he's not Tallence," she whispered, suddenly frightened again. "Oh, Simon, where is he? What will he do next?"

He paused before replying, and when he spoke it was as if he had spent much time in secret thought before coming to the conclusion he now confided in her.

"I don't think he is going to do much at all. I think he intends only to tease me. In time, he'll tire of it."

Then, he kissed her passionately, as if wishing to forget all his outside worries, and with a sigh, she yielded, her whole being afire with her desire for him.

Despite the heat which came with the dawn that next morning, she slept on peacefully, to be awakened about eight by a pale-faced Lily.

"Mrs. Sandford," said the servant, her voice strained by the most fearful anxiety, "you must get up at once. The children have vanished."

14

CURWOOD homestead was not an especially large house, although when it had been built, in the years prior to the discovery of gold, it had been quite grand by pioneer standards. Already, Jane and her husband had earnestly discussed extensions, for, with the arrival of their own family, existing accommodation would be inadequate for the standards expected of the well-to-do.

While Chloris McFarlane had been with them, Rodney's bedroom had had to double as a day nursery and wet-weather schoolroom. The small room occupied by Miss McFarlane separated the small boy's quarters from those of his sister, and because it was more convenient until the new governess arrived, Rodney had been moved, for the time being, next door to his sister.

These two particular rooms looked out over the roof of the servants' single storey quarters and that of the kitchen, which, following the usual early Australian custom, was in a building separate from the main house. Inside, they opened directly on to the passage at the head of the stairs. The senior Sandfords slept in the large bedroom at the front of the house, extending across the full width, being separated from the currently empty room by a linen and sewing room.

On the other side of the stairwell ran a passage against the wall, with two windows for extra light, so that the whole plan, which gave the impression of a house chopped into two, revealed that the original owners, the Parkers, had intended eventually to enlarge the building.

When Lily told Jane that the children were missing she did not take the news very seriously. After all, she and Simon slept no more than a few yards from Dolly and Rodney.

"They must have slipped out early," she yawned, "and I expect the heat woke them up soon after dawn. They're probably playing outside."

"Oh no, Mrs. Sandford. Not in their nightclothes."

Dolly took pride in dressing herself, and could help her little brother to do the same, if not very competently.

"Oh dear!"

Jane, at this point, was sure that the whole thing was a fuss over nothing, and rather grumpily, for she was annoyed with herself for oversleeping, she pulled on her light robe and went to investigate. The children's beds had undoubtedly been slept in. In Rodney's room, his favourite bedtime toy, a sawdust-filled creature of vaguely canine derivation, which he called Wooffy, lay on the floor, as if spilled there as its owner climbed out of bed. In Dolly's room, her beloved Christabel was primly in her own little cot, tucked in neatly under her own tiny mosquito net.

"Haven't you gone outside and called to them?" Jane mentally arranged to give the pair a good talking-to when the time came. "Really, they've run quite wild since Miss McFarlane left."

Lily sent her a long, sour look, as if to say, "And whose fault is that?"

Aloud, her reply was exasperated.

"Of course, I've called out to them,"

254

she snapped. "We've been out looking for the past half an hour. There's no sign of them, and no one's seen them, not this morning, anyway."

Simon came upstairs at this moment, and his face was anxious.

"There's no sign of them still," he stated. Then he came to his young wife, and took both her hands. "Jane," he continued, "there's something very wrong. The ladder from the stables was lying out in the yard."

So saying, he pulled her to the window and pointed out into the back yard beyond the servants' quarters, and it was at this moment that Jane began to feel the grip of terror.

"No one needed it here yesterday. I think someone climbed up during the night and took them. The front door was open when I went down this morning, just after dawn."

Against all evidence, she still had to argue, as much to convince herself that this terrible thing could not have happened as to contradict him.

"How could anyone carry two children downstairs without either of them waking and crying out?" she demanded.

"Jane!" he shouted, losing his temper. "Don't you understand? *My* children have vanished. My children!"

It was the first time he had ever raised his voice to her, and she drew back, shocked into realising that simple, logical explanations would not do. Lily, who was still hovering in the background, now spoke up and told Jane that she had checked carefully through the children's clothes. They had still to be in their night attire.

"Wait until I dress."

Normally, Lily would have helped her, but Jane waved her away with the brusque remark that she could dress herself and Lily had best continue searching for that pair of young imps. She forced herself to say that last, to try to keep up their spirits.

Never had her fingers been so clumsy, or hooks so difficult to fit into eyes. And her hair! A few strokes with the heavy silver-backed brush and a quick twist prodded through with hairpins had to suffice.

Before going downstairs, Jane looked

out of the window, above and across the garden, past the picket gate, and down the wide, dusty slope to the river, concealed by trees and shrubbery. She shuddered and tried to quell the new fear which permeated her mind. It could be so very easy. The smaller child slipping into a deep pool, the older, larger child trying vainly to pull the little one to safety and being dragged down by the other's struggles.

Closer to hand, Charlie Hung, the gardener, was already at work watering the small plants he had set out a few days previously on her own insistence, for the seedsman in Sandhurst had advised her that autumn planting was necessary for early spring results. Yesterday, the plants had been pathetically limp and on the point of perishing. So much for your Australian seasons, she thought, crossly. This is autumn, they claim, but the wretched heat goes on day after day. No wonder the children wake up early and decide on pranks.

This was the explanation, she insisted to Simon. The little scamps were hiding somewhere, intent on plaguing their elders as much out of boredom as from mischief. The ladder in the yard was pure coincidence. Someone had brought it over yesterday, and having forgotten to restore it to its rightful place, decided not to own to the fault.

The search continued and spread. Every shed and outhouse and loft was searched. Lily and Charlie Hung went down to the river, Lily somehow overcoming language difficulties and explaining to the Chinese that he must probe the last few remaining deep pools with a pole.

By nine o'clock, in an increasing oppressiveness which had already frayed tempers, every logical place had been explored, and Simon sent one of the men off to Omega, where two aboriginal shepherds were employed, with orders for them to come to Curwood as quickly as possible.

"If anyone can find them, those blacks will," he explained tersely. "A blackfellow can follow a trail where you or I see nothing."

Then he swung himself up on to Bevis, and rode off at full gallop towards the

258

valley where the Wells family lived. Whatever the strains between the two households, lost children in the Australian bush always brought about a temporary unity of effort. Jane thought despairingly of the many old shafts and pits in that desolate valley. What would have possessed young children to venture off in that direction so early in the day?

She went into the outside schoolroom under the veranda roof at the side of the house, in the forlorn hope that here there might be, a clue to the children's whereabouts. There was nothing out of place, and as she turned, she glanced at the thermometer. It was not as high as she had expected, yet, on this morning, in the clean, bright sunshine, the air was so heavy that ordinary movement was exhausting. For a second, she felt dizzy, and braced herself with a hand against the nearest wall. It was not the first time this had happened recently, and although until now she had dismissed it as a result of worries and fears, she felt a flutter of hope.

Not so long ago, she had scorned Lily's suggestion that she might be pregnant.

Suddenly, despite the anxieties of the morning, she welcomed the possibility with joy.

Then she found herself confronted by Lily, who held out a sheet of paper, such as may have been torn from an exercise book.

"Charlie found this on the bench where Dolly plays," said the older woman, simply. "I think Mr. Sandford was right, after all. Someone has taken the children. Is there anyone you can send off to fetch the troopers?"

('Trooper' was the Australian name for a mounted policeman, harking back to earlier times when soldiers assisted in upholding the law.)

Quickly, Jane read the message which was printed boldly across the paper.

"Sandford. Come to the high rises above the flume and we'll talk. Bring your wife so there is no funny business. J. Tallence."

Lily was talking again, and Jane collected herself sufficiently to listen. This must be a dream, she kept thinking, like the nightmare which had so shaken her on her first night at Curwood.

260

"Mrs. Wells was lying, all right," said Lily, grimly. "That was not her no-good brother, Mrs. Sandford. That was Jack Tallence all along, like you said." She took a deep breath, as if to calm herself. "Now, I haven't spoken of this before, knowing it would upset you and Mr. Sandford, but the little girl's a sharp child, and she has a long memory. She can remember her mother quite well, and her Uncle James Parker from the time before, and the man she calls Uncle Jack. She liked Uncle Jack. It seems he used to make a great fuss of her, and tell her all sorts of stories about elephants and tigers and princes and princesses, and a lot of other outlandish nonsense. Inflaming her poor little brain, if you ask me. It's my idea, he's managed to speak to her recently, and told her to leave the house and bring her brother to him. That's why neither of 'em cried out. I know it's forbidden ground, Mrs. Sandford, but it stands to reason he would like to see the little boy. You have to admit there's not much of Mr. Sandford in young Rodney."

"Please, Lily," implored Jane. "Give

me the paper, and let me think for a little while."

The two women walked into the house together, and Jane saw herself reflected in the tall mirror which had recently been installed in the hallway to give an illusion of spaciousness. Already, she was flushed with heat and quite haggard, and the flowered cotton dress she had donned freshly that morning was limp and crumpled.

"Lily," she said, trying to fight her way out of the labyrinth of conflicting facts, "how could a stranger enter our front garden and place that note on the bench without being seen?"

"I don't know that, Mrs. Sandford." The other's round face was suddenly very smooth and expressionless, as if a door had closed.

Jane studied her servant thoughtfully. It was strange, but until this instant, she had never realised just how little she knew about Lily. Lily Fields had been with her Aunt Dorcas for several years, but Lily might have sprung into the world by a sort of spontaneous miracle for all Jane knew about her background. Was it possible that she had been transported? Transportation was a thing of the past in eastern Australia, but it had ceased only during the early part of that same decade when continual protests from the Australasian League to the British Government had stopped the flow of convicts to Van Diemen's Land. That island colony, eager to shake off its brutal past, had promptly changed its name to Tasmania. Transportation to mainland eastern Australia had halted nearly twenty years since, but Lily was about forty, and quite old enough to have 'come out under hatches'. Or, perhaps, were her parents amongst those thousands upon thousands who had, in the jargon of the felons, made the long voyage to Australia 'legally'?

"There's always a lot of coming and going about this place, Mrs. Sandford," said Lily, after a longish pause, as if she felt she was obliged to offer an explanation. "Specially since Mr. Sandford has taken over Omega. I don't know half the fellows I see about the men's quarters. At first, I did know most of them, by sight anyway, because a lot of 'em aren't exactly the sort I'd mix with. But some have left, and there's new faces, and as I said, all this coming and going from over at Omega."

Jane felt that she had to be alone for a few minutes, and sent Lily off to fetch her some tea. While she was waiting, she went upstairs again, and gazed out of her bedroom window, with its wide view, The sunlight, she noticed, was no longer so clear, but had a slightly yellowish tinge. Then, restlessly, she walked into Dolly's room, and peered through the window across the roof of the servants' quarters to the back yard with its clothes lines and dog kennel.

The watchdog, a black brute of indefinite breed which she detested, would not have dozed silently whilst an intruder propped up a ladder and climbed up across the wood-shingled roof in order to hoist himself up into Dolly's room. It was, in fact, hard to imagine anyone except a circus acrobat accomplishing such a deed. The presence of the ladder at the rear of the house was, as she had insisted, a coincidence. Lily's idea, that the children had left of their own volition to meet someone they knew, was quite logical.

Jack Tallence must be a veritable Pied Piper, she thought. Unless — had the children been taken out by someone else? The woman they trusted and ran to in preference to their stepmother?

It must be Lily! It must have been Lily all along. Who else could have stolen the letter — to show Jack Tallence? — and placed the necklace, given to her by the same man, on the bench? How easy it had been for Lily to say that she had found that terrifying note on the bench.

Jane returned downstairs, and sat down to drink her tea, remembering belatedly that in the confusion she had omitted to have breakfast. She was hungry now, but the butter on the thin slices of bread which had come with the tea was slightly rancid. She was about to ring the bell and ask for biscuits when Simon returned. He looked exhausted, and sank down on to the nearest chair, drawing a hand wearily across his forehead.

He had, he said, ridden across country, and spoken to Joe Wells. Joe Wells, and the two eldest boys, George and Tom, were now out scouring the valley for any sign of the children. He had told her this before she showed him the note. He stared at it, apparently bemused, and demanded to know where she had found it. She explained the details of its discovery.

"But that's impossible! How could he come to the house? In broad daylight?"

He had always disliked Lily, and she found it hard to impart to him her suspicions. What would Papa have said? There was a quotation from the Psalms, something about mine own familiar friend, in whom I trusted. For Jane, Lily had been more than a servant. She had been a friend, a prop, someone with whom she had shared deep sorrow, and the source of virtually the only disagreements Jane had had with her husband.

Haltingly, and in a low voice, she told him what she had surmised, and he seemed almost unable to comprehend.

"Lily?"

It was obvious that the shocks of the day had hit him hard, and he was quite unaware of the smudges of dust across his nose and cheeks where it had stuck to perspiration.

"Oh, Simon, it must be. Who else? I mean, she's the one who has helped Jack Tallence all along."

He gulped down his tea.

"We'll deal with her later," he said, after a few moments. "For now, we must go to the stony rises as he says. If he wants to bargain, that must be the way of it."

"Simon! Shouldn't we send for the troopers? He's a madman. We can't go there without any protection. You know how those rocks dominate the landscape for miles about. He could shoot you as you approach. Please, we must think of a plan. We could send some of the men to move up on him from behind."

He was like a man in a trance. The brooding quality in his features which had so attracted her at the first had now intensified, so that he was remote from her, hardly hearing what she had said.

"They're my children, Jane. I'll take any risk for them. Always remember that, If you won't come, I'll go alone."

She knew then that she had to

accompany him. Her presence was his protection as well as Tallence's.

"All right, Simon. But I'll need my hat. I'll only be a few minutes."

Upstairs, she splashed her hot face with water, as much to quieten her trembling nerves as to cool herself, but once again, her fingers shook as she tried to fasten the ribbons of her wide-brimmed hat under her chin. Lily, at first unnoticed, had come quietly into the room.

"Don't go, Mrs. Sandford," she said, severely, and then reverted to the familiarity of their earlier days together. "Please, Miss Jane. It's men's work. Don't put yourself in danger."

"The note told us both to come. Oh, Lily, one must do what one can for the children."

With the greatest of surprise, she saw the tears rolling down Lily's cheeks. Half an hour before, she had been ready to condemn the other as a villainness, and then she thought she understood. Lily hated Simon Sandford. Whatever she had done had been to hurt him, not his wife.

"Lily," she said, severely, "if you have

anything to say to me, please say it now."

Lily looked blank at first, and then held out her hand to Jane. On her palm was a pistol, the tiniest weapon Jane had ever imagined. She had had very little experience of firearms, having a healthy fear of such things, and she was startled.

"Take it with you, Miss Jane. I bought it in a second-hand place down in Melbourne before we came up to Curwood the first time. It's a lady's pistol. You can hide it in your pocket."

"I couldn't use such a thing!"

"It's loaded, but quite safe until you cock it," said Lily, and quickly explained how this was done.

Jane made up her mind.

"Thank you. I'll take it." And not tell Simon, she added, silently. He may trust Tallence, but I do not.

Outside, Simon was waiting with the horse and light vehicle which had borne her and Lily to the Wells place on the previous day. Yesterday, debating what to do about Jack O'Shea, she had been troubled by conscience-provoking memories of her extraordinary life with Papa. Today, Papa's misdeeds were no longer relevant, and indeed, were trivial compared against the sheer evil generated by the sequence of mystifying events here at Curwood.

Simon helped her up on to her seat without a word. His features were set into resolution, and at this time he was so obviously disinclined to talk that Jane kept her thoughts to herself.

All that wretched morning, a particular truth had been eluding her, but as Simon touched his whip to the horse to move the sluggish beast into a rattling trot, she grasped at it from the recesses of her mind.

There was no sense to it.

In effect, as far as she was concerned, the whole thing had commenced on that morning when she had stood on the deck of the *Kincardine*, a plain, lovesick girl longing for a last glimpse of the man she adored. How vividly the tableau recreated itself now, Simon and his family, and the obnoxious Mrs. O'Brien and hers, grouped amidst the bustling confusion on Railway Pier. Just as vivid in her mind's eye was the approaching stranger she later knew as James Parker, caught in an off guard moment by the watcher from the ship.

The key to the puzzle had to be that Tallence and James Parker were in partnership.

But the young woman who had learned to think quickly and clearly under the necessity of living with Papa was not satisfied. Emotion wanted to link the two men in villainy, but reason demurred.

Revenge? But Simon was the wronged party in the sad triangle of love and betrayal involving himself, Tallence and foolish Sarah.

Money? Tallence could not hope to gain financially from Simon's death, and neither could Parker, unless the plotters envisaged no less than four deaths, Simon's, her own, and the children's. But, in this ghastly eventuality, Caleb, and possibly the Parker parents, elderly but still alive in New Zealand, could presumably lay claim to part of the estate. No, that had to be dismissed as pure fantasy.

She dealt with other ridiculous notions,

such as buried treasure under the floorboards at Curwood, with the same methodical calm.

The only solution was that Tallence was hopelessly deranged, and this finally made nonsense of any theory that the Wells family were hiding him under the guise of Jack O'Shea. It also threw doubt upon the probability of James Parker's involvement. She did not like the man, but the very lack of emotion which had annoyed her could also indicate that he would have no qualms about having an insane friend quietly locked away.

Oddly, she did not feel particularly frightened as they moved towards their appointment with the phantom who would soon assume solid form and reveal himself to them both.

In the happy years which lay ahead, Jane would come to liken how she felt on that oppressive morning at Curwood to her sensations as labour pains commenced. There was no going back: the time of reckoning had come. For good or for bad, it had to be suffered through to the end.

15

SEVERAL hundred yards from the homestead, the track forked, the branch to the left leading travellers along the lower side of the valley where the Wells family dwelt, and the one to the right passing through the forested area where Jane and Simon had picnicked together on that wonderful, carefree day when he had first taken her into his arms and whispered to her of his desire for her. The left branch was also the road which led to the nearest township, and if either of the Sandfords had looked back over their shoulders as they turned right, they would have seen two horsemen approaching.

Both, naturally, were too absorbed in what lay ahead to notice, and the two horsemen, intent on reaching the homestead, did not see them as they passed out of sight behind trees.

Lily, her face still stained with the tears which had softened Jane's suspicions,

273

saw them as they dismounted outside the picket gate and hitched their horses to the posts provided for that purpose. Immediately, she ran out, the ribbons of her little cap streaming behind her head.

"Oh, Mr. Parker," she cried, "I can't believe it's you. I thought you'd gone back to New Zealand. It's the answer to a prayer, that's what it is."

Parker smiled, rather thinly.

"I hadn't expected such a welcome," he said. "Lily, allow me to introduce this gentleman. He came to see Mrs. Sandford, but he would like a word with you first."

The other man was big, with wide-apart eyes and a fair complexion, and at this moment, both hot and sunburnt, for his arrival in Victoria had been so recent that he had had little chance to acclimatize himself to this late spell of hot weather.

Lily shook her head, trying to find the words to explain all that had happened, and Parker spoke again.

"This is Mr. Evan Whiteside, Lily, formerly of the London police force, but now a new recruit in the Victoria Police."

274

"Miss Fields," said Whiteside, gravely, "I have reason to believe that Mrs. Sandford is not what she seems."

"You mean that she kidnapped the children?" demanded Lily, incredulously. "My Miss Jane? Oh no, you must be wrong, sir."

"Kidnapped?" Parker reached out and gripped the woman's forearm. "What do you mean? What has happened here today?"

The yellow tinge which Jane had observed earlier in the sunlight had deepened. Shadows were no longer black but a pale brown, blurring into disappearance. Yet there were no clouds visible in the sky, no thunderheads promising relief from the heavy humidity.

Lily began to weep, blurting out a fairly incoherent account of what had happened.

"Is Mrs. Sandford here?" Whiteside was curt, and the very harshness of his tone had a calming effect on Lily. "Now, listen to me for a moment. I believe that Mrs. Sandford is a young woman I knew in England as Jenny Turner. It is of the utmost importance that Mr. Parker and

275

I talk with her. What we have to tell her could save her life!"

"But she's gone, with Mr. Sandford, to talk to that crazy Mr. Tallence who has taken the children. That's what I've been trying to tell you, Mr. Parker. I don't know anything about Jenny Turner."

"Tallence?" Parker's voice was a whipcrack. "Where?"

Lily told him about the note, and Whiteside visibly gritted his teeth.

"Our horses are worn out. We've ridden up from Melbourne. They're too far ahead for us to catch them up."

* * *

Jane and her husband exchanged no more than a dozen words as they jolted over the track which rounded the head of the valley before ascending the ridge towards the high point where the great boulders formed a landmark. In contrast to the green grass, blue skies and cool breeze of the wonderful day when Simon had proposed to her, the whole landscape was brown, and the air of a hot stillness. The yellow tinge in the sky Jane had

276

noticed earlier had intensified, and when she remarked upon it, Sandford's answer was one, laconic word.

"Dust."

His tone was so sharp that she preferred to remain silent as the vehicle rattled and jolted over the pitted track. Through the timbered stretch they passed, the wheels crackling over small fallen branches and lengths of twisted bark which had peeled away from tree trunks.

A magpie, that large, crow-shaped bird of black and white feathering which had been given a name familiar to English immigrants, was poking about with its sharp white bill on the track, and fluttered away almost from beneath the horse's hooves, either too short-sighted or absent-minded to see danger approach. But, other than that, there was no life visible. It was as if all the birds and small creatures of the bushland were in hiding until the relief of rain. In the spring, there had been wild flowers, small and modest by European standards, but in great variety and colour. Today, there was nought but sere stalks and dusty, thorny shrubbery, and drought-hardened earth littered with gum tree refuse.

A dreadful landscape for a dreadful day, she thought, as they left the trees behind and began the ascent on the Whipstick side of the valley. The only patch of green was below the Wells' shack, where water from the flume irrigated their vegetables. The rest of that devastated place was glaringly white and yellow, a waste of exposed clay and subsoil dried to dust.

The two crows fluttered away as Simon Sandford reined in the horse before the last, very steep section of the track. How did the gloomy old ballad go?

"I wot there lies a newslain Knight;
And naebody kens that he lies there,
But his hawk, his hound, and lady fair."

Two crows, 'The Twa Corbies', telling a tale of medieval passion and betrayal, feeding on the poor, dead knight whilst his faithless wife and her new lover enjoyed themselves! It was so apt that it had to be a warning.

"No!" cried Jane, as Simon made

to assist her down from the cart, "we mustn't go any further. It's a trap. A horrid trick. He'll shoot you. Please, Simon, let's go back. We'll bring men. We mustn't do this stupid thing."

"It's too late," he responded, in a monotone. His face was a set mask. "I have to do this, Jane. Come along."

At first, she sat defiantly, refusing to move, for she hoped to make him see reason and return to Curwood.

"If Joe Wells and his sons are out looking for the children in the valley," she said, "Tallence could have been scared away."

In reply, he pointed up towards the great jumbled pile of rocks, and she saw a figure standing there. Tallence!

The haze had deepened. She looked down at the ground as she climbed out of the cart, and saw that their shadows had vanished. The sun had become a reddish orb in the orange sky, and she shuddered so violently that she had to stand still in an effort to control herself. She wanted to turn and run from this evil place, for all the happiness she had connected with these rocks had evaporated into fear.

"I'm quite safe," said Sandford, taking her arm. "Believe that, Jane."

But she hardly heard him. She was staring down and across the valley, to the Wells' shack. How strange! No smoke came from the chimney, no washing hung from the clothes-lines, and no sound of life floated in the quiet, still air.

"Simon!" She uttered each word clearly and slowly, hardly able to believe herself what she was saying. "I think the Wells family have gone. They must have left after you spoke to them this morning."

He did not answer, but tugged at her arm. She pulled away, for instinct made her wish to walk wide of her husband, in the hope of making them jointly a more difficult target. Lily's little pistol weighed heavily in her pocket, and she prayed for the courage to use it if the necessity arose.

At the same time, she could not overlook the sudden departure of the Wells family, motivated, she was positive, by her probings into the identity of the mysterious extra man.

"Listen to me," she said, in a low,

hushed, but insistent voice. "I think the Wells family took Dolly and Rodney with them. Simon, it makes sense. The boy Tom knows Curwood well, and the children know him, too. The whole tribe must have left immediately after you spoke to them."

Why would he not listen?

"They must have been in league with Tallence all along. Such a shady character could have known O'Shea — perhaps they even worked together. It explains everything, Simon. Tallence has been blackmailing Jack O'Shea into helping him. We must go back to Curwood homestead straight away. The Wells family cannot have moved far, and such a crowd must be easily traced. There's no need to risk ourselves now, Simon. Don't you understand?"

Sandford still ignored her. The figure ahead had separated itself from the rocks, and was quite easy to see, in spite of the false dusk settling so early in the day. Jane's first thought, puzzling and clarifying at the same time, was that this was definitely not the man she had seen darting back into the mine.

The person was rather stocky, wearing smart riding clothes which were topped by a wide-brimmed hat with a red silk scarf bound about the crown, with the ends dropping down at the back to form a puggaree, this neck protection being called, inelegantly, a 'poultice'.

There was a peremptory wave of a surprisingly small gloved hand, ordering them to approach, and Jane heard her husband draw a deep breath as he quickened his steps.

So, this was Jack Tallence, Sarah's lover and the kidnapper of Sarah's children. In the midst of her fear and puzzlement, Jane could only think that he was both shorter and plumper than she had expected. Sarah, she knew from references to the fact that Dolly was growing tall, like her mother, had been above average female height, to match her lanky twin, James. That she should have chosen to elope with this somewhat pudgy and dandified person was surprising, to say the least of it.

Sandford reached out and grabbed her by the arm, with a firmness which made her wince and cry out.

"Come on. We've wasted too much time." His voice was rough, and his fingers pressed into her arm savagely so that she could feel pressure against the bone.

"Hullo!" It was not a man's voice at all, and with a bravado gesture, the wide-brimmed hat was swept off, and the shining black, smoothly brilliantined locks of Mrs. Honora O'Brien were revealed.

"Mrs. O'Brien! Is this your idea of a joke?"

Even as she spoke, Jane knew that there was no joke intended. The whole grotesque affair was in earnest, with Sandford part of it.

"Simon," continued Mrs. O'Brien, as if Jane had not spoken, "I thought you would never come. It is so fearfully hot up here, and the ants are so bad I couldn't even sit down."

Jane wrenched her arm free of Sandford's grasp.

"Where's Jack Tallence?" she demanded. Inside her mind, a battle was raging. Sense told her that Simon was her enemy, but love, loathe to die, tried to convince her that somehow, incredibly,

Mrs. O'Brien was in league with the shadowy Jack Tallence. "And where are the children?"

"Oh, the children will be found in good time," cried the widow, quite gaily, her confidence reinforced by the workmanlike pistol she held steadily in her right hand. "As for Jack Tallence — Simon and I built him up out of nothing just for the purpose of getting rid of you. How nasty he was to poor Simon, spreading all those horrid stories; And sneaking in and out of your house! Tch, tch! But when he's killed you, quite by accident, because you'll throw yourself in front of your husband to save him, naughty Jack will be gone, and poor Simon will be a sorrowing widower again, poor, dear man."

For a second, Jane thought that she was going to faint. She felt physically ill with disbelief. Her husband, her adoring husband, who had swept her off her feet, was the instigator of all the mysteries and petty torments. He had stolen the letter (forged?), he had left the necklace where Dolly could find it, cleverly placing the blame on innocent Chloris McFarlane, and without a doubt, had made up the story about the shot fired at him by Tallence.

"Why should you do this to me, Simon?" she implored, looking up into his implacably closed face. "And what can you hope to gain from it?" she added, turning to Mrs. O'Brien.

"I wish to marry Honora," said Sandford, simply, as if saying that he would like lamb cutlets for dinner.

"But why didn't you? You could have, if you hadn't married me?" Odd, how ordinary were the processes of her thinking at this time. This wicked and scheming pair meant to murder her, but she felt entitled to know exactly why.

"Honora's money is tied up in a trust. When she remarries, she is penniless."

"But you're a wealthy man, Simon." Now it was becoming clearer. The love of money, as Papa had so often quoted, is the root of all evil. This man, this familiar friend who was her secret foe, wanted her own fortune, to add to his own.

"Alas, Jane, I'm not wealthy." His face

wore that slight and sad smile which she had always found so enchanting. "I left England because I'd run out of funds and I was in debt. Honora and I didn't travel together because we wished to protect her reputation."

Out of the corner of her eye, Jane saw that a decidedly impatient expression was settling on Mrs. O'Brien's coarsely handsome features, and she resisted the temptation to ask what reputation.

"I soon discovered," continued Sandford, "that there was an heiress on board the *Kincardine*, but she was too well protected. Until fate stepped in and made her eager to turn to me for help. Then that dragon, Lily Fields, did her best to chase me away, and when you left Melbourne so suddenly, Jane, I thought she'd succeeded. But Caleb told me you'd written to him asking his help in finding a new manager, and I could hardly credit my luck."

"But you said . . . " Jane's voice trailed away. Obviously, Simon was a consummate and inveterate liar. His disarming tale of coming to Curwood to enquire whether she would sell the property to him was just another falsehood.

"Stop wasting time with talk. Come on, Plain Jane," sneered Mrs. O'Brien, handling the pistol in a very professional manner. "I want you in amongst the rocks. I think Simon would be happier if he didn't see your last moment."

I don't want to die, thought Jane, quite matter-of-factly. What would Papa have done? Her mind fled back across occasions when necessity had prompted a quiet exit from lodgings, which however humble, were usually presided over by a vigilant landlady. The diversion. That was the pivot of the technique. There had been a few useful ploys.

The face at the window caused confusion in the more genteel establishment, giving Papa time to remove their small amount of baggage from under that roof. Similarly, a maidenly faint had been known to work wonders, although it was quite useless in those venues where a hint that the peelers were on their way was more relevant.

It was strange how, in such a little time, so much flooded through her

287

mind. There was the occasion when they had been very comfortably settled, with no immediate money worries, and they had been awakened in the night by the most frightful commotion emanating from the floor above. Another lodger had killed his wife, and while everyone else was screaming and running about and calling for the police to come, she and Papa had quickly packed and left. Later, they read in the newspaper that the husband had believed his wife to have a lover, a suspicion which was tragically unfounded.

"'The ear of jealousy," said Papa sadly, "'heareth all things.'"

At the same time, another revelation came to Jane. Simon, whom she had always thought to be so strong and reliable, was the weaker one in this unholy partnership.

"Mrs. O'Brien, didn't you feel jealous when you thought about Simon and I? He has been husband to me in every way. There has been no pretence."

"Shut up!" Honora's raw nerve was touched, and her eyes left Jane for the first time. "He's never loved you! Never!"

she screeched, but she was looking at Sandford.

Jane's right hand slid down into her pocket.

"Simon," she said, very softly, "has it all been pretence?"

"Jane, for God's sake, just do as she says." He was faltering. Now that the time had come, he was not as strong-stomached as Honora O'Brien.

"If you kill me, you kill two people."

Everything seemed to have slowed down, and voices were echoing hollowly in the hot and turgid air. Yet, her statement startled both the conspirators, and gave Jane the few seconds she needed.

"No!" Honora O'Brien spat out the word. "You're lying. Simon, don't listen to her. She's trying to trick you."

"Hon, look out. My God, she's got a pistol!"

Jane, hardly knowing what she was doing, cocked, aimed and fired. The sharp little report was followed by a scream from Honora O'Brien, who dropped her own weapon as she clutched at her thigh. Through the stuff of her riding breeches, a few inches above the left knee, blood seeped out.

"Kill her, kill her," screamed the woman, and Sandford jumped at Jane, who, amazed that the tiny toy could have hurt anyone, was standing quite still.

A reflex action, rather than a conscious effort, made her dodge the man, and then she slipped, landing in a sitting position, and skidded down, painfully and terrifyingly. To her left was the spring which everlastingly fed the flume, and she somehow managed to halt her descent by grabbing at the wooden half-box which carried the water across the deepest part of the valley to the primitive machinery used by Joe Wells.

Sobbing, she lay there, water gushing down on to her, until a fall of earth and rock fragments warned her to look up, and she saw Simon carefully lowering himself. His expression warned her that his time of indecision had passed. He knew that he had to kill her to protect himself.

16

TO the northwest, the sky had blackened, and for the first time that day, a breeze stirred. It was not a cooling or refreshing zephyr, but akin to the puff of hot air from a partly opened stove door. Partly soaked as she was, Jane still perspired profusely, so much that, not daring to look down, she had to hang on to her precarious perch with one hand whilst she wiped away the droplets trickling into her eyes.

Those moments when she had been thinking so clearly up there near the rocks had gone. All she felt now was a dull panic and an animal desire to survive. If Simon has Honora's pistol, she thought, I'll be dead before I've moved a yard, but even so, she did the only thing possible. She began crawling along the aqueduct.

Once, she did try to stand up in the narrow channel, but vertigo overcame her, and she continued crawling, knees

291

dragging through the water, hands being scratched raw by the rough edges of the wooden sides. The timber was soaked so thoroughly that it was waterproofed, like a wooden bucket or wash trough, but it was also slimy and splintery. She did not venture to look down, only straight ahead, towards the Wells mine and puddling machine so far away that she felt that she could never reach them. Sandford began crawling behind her, and the added weight made the whole structure creak and sway dangerously, for down on the valley floor, white ants had damaged the bases of many of the uprights.

"Hell and damnation!"

At the uttered curse, she risked a second to glance back. He did have the pistol, but had somehow dropped it into the water, and he had paused to shake out the moisture, setting the whole makeshift structure trembling again. Then, he aimed and pressed the trigger. At this instant, she was still looking at him, so frightened that she could neither move nor utter even a squeak, waiting for the thud of the bullet into her body, half-wanting the end so that she could escape this continuing horror.

The weapon misfired, and with another curse, he tossed it aside, and again began crawling towards her. His body being unhampered by the skirts which wound themselves about her legs, he made rapid progress. God had spared her so far: she had to act. Almost holding her breath so that she would not move too much, she managed to pull off one shoe. Comforting her whole body in the effort, she flung it back at Sandford. It was a lucky shot, hitting him on the side of the face, and for a moment or two, he was off balance, and she crawled on as fast as she was able, increasing the distance between them, temporarily, at least.

She was about halfway across when the first gust of wind hit. Her hat, still ludicrously tied by its ribbons, flapped wildly, and she had to undo it, so that it blew away, rising and falling until it vanished from sight. At the same time, grit and small rubbish, twigs and leaves and the like, stung her face, catching in her hair which now blew about, its pins loosening and dropping out as her hat flew off. Just as unexpectedly, the wind dropped, and she heard clearly, from up high, at the base of the rocks, above the spring, Mrs. O'Brien's voice called out frantically.

"Simon! Simon! Come back!"

Honora O'Brien, from her vantage point, could see that which was still invisible to the pair on the flume. A huge cloud, brown and swirling and yet, for all its size, strangely compact, was funnelling towards the valley, a wind storm which sucked and discharged debris as it moved.

Then the woman's voice became a fading whistle against the wind. Until now, Jane had not dared look down in case she was overwhelmed by giddiness. Therefore, she did not realise that she had passed the deepest part of the valley and that she was no more than fifteen feet above the ground. She was aware only of the man who was now about five yards behind her, and she felt her breath becoming more laboured with each movement. Her whole body hurt from her fall, her knees were agonising patches of rawness, her hands bled from a myriad scratches and splinters. She had to stop. She could not move another inch until she had rested.

The man was quick to take advantage of her weariness. He edged closer, and reached out towards her, grabbing the hem of her torn skirts.

"I'm going to break your stupid neck," Sandford said, for he was in a rage of fear and desperation at the way in which he had misjudged his outwardly compliant and demure young wife.

There was a roaring in her ears. She seemed to be going blind. Everything was dark and suffocating, and the flume jolted beneath her.

"Jump down, Jenny. Jump for your life!"

She was dying. She had to be. Evan Whiteside's voice, floating in from the past, was proof of that. But he was there in solid flesh, to her right and below, holding up his arms to her, and at his side was James Parker.

It was a last effort. Somehow, with a ripping of cloth, she pulled away from Sandford's clutch, and thudded downwards, feeling the strong hands which caught her and broke her fall.

"Run!" James Parker's shout was almost obliterated by the din.

She was too exhausted to move, and the two men half carried, half dragged her away from the collapsing flume, to a pit left by the miners who had ruined this valley. As they lay down, the storm whirled and sucked and tossed and discarded all about them. Once, she felt her body being lifted, and Whiteside flung himself across her, forcing himself down with every ounce of his bulky strength.

It was all over in an incredibly short time. The noise and the dirt and darkness had travelled on, carried forward by the velocity of the monstrous freak wind which charged off relentlessly, changing course suddenly to exhaust itself across the wastes of the Whipstick.

The flume was now nothing but two pathetic broken frames, one on either side of the valley. The rest was scattered for hundreds of yards, shattered grey poles and scraps of splintered wood fit for nothing but burning. The Wells' shack had simply disappeared, but in the ridiculous way of such storms, the puddling machine, the outdoor toilet, and a fowl shed had been spared. A hen, dead and half stripped of its feathers, had landed in the pit in which the trio had sheltered, and after throwing the corpse aside, Parker scrambled up and stared about him.

"I've heard of such things," he said, slowly and disbelievingly, "but I'd no idea of what they were like. Are you both all right?"

Whiteside had also clambered to his feet, and was dusting himself down, while Jane, supported by James Parker, could utter only two words.

"Where's Simon?"

What had happened in the hour prior to the storm had been temporarily wiped from her mind, and all she could think of as she looked about her at the wreckage was that somewhere Simon must be lying, perhaps injured. He was her husband, and her love. Where was he?

Parker and Whiteside wanted her to leave the place, but she insisted that they search. Parker found him after a few minutes, and quickly removed his coat and partly covered the dead man. Jane screamed and demanded to see Simon, but they relentlessly forced her away.

Sandford's body was badly crushed, and his face, the brooding face with its strange power over women, was almost unrecognisable. Later, at the inquest, the doctor who had examined him testified that it was his belief that Mr. Sandford's neck had been broken as he was thrown from the flume by the fury of the wind.

Curwood homestead, spared in the great fire of 1851, was not so lucky this time. The roof had been ripped from the main part of the house, and every single pane of glass had been smashed by enormous hailstones which had been dropped, fairly patchily, by the tornado. Jane was carried to Lily's little room in the servants' quarters, which were relatively intact, and she sank into a merciful unconsciousness, aided by laudanum drops fortuitously produced by Lily.

Her first question, when she awoke many hours later, was whether the children had been found. The answer was yes. The poor little dears were tucked up in bed themselves and sound asleep after their ordeal.

Tom Wells had brought them home, footsore and utterly worn out, about an hour before sunset. He was very tired himself, having carried Rodney for several miles on his back.

The Wells family had decided to leave after Jane's visit. Tom did not explain the exact reason, but it was clearly involved with the necessity for Dancing Jack O'Shea to find another refuge. They had simply packed everything they could into their wagon and went off, trailing after the vehicle on foot, setting up camp in the open air overnight.

About midday, the party stopped for their midday meal, near what they had thought to be a deserted cottage left by a miner who had moved on elsewhere. To their surprise, when he and Uncle Jack walked past the cottage on their way to a well which they knew to be there, they heard children crying out.

Uncle Jack sent Tom to investigate, keeping himself out of sight, for whatever they say, said Tom defiantly, Uncle Jack's allus had a soft spot for little 'uns.

"Could 'a' knocked me backwards with a feather, Mrs. Sandford! Little Miss Dolly and young Roddy, weeping their eyes out at bein' left all alone in that cottage. Not that the cottage was so bad inside. Someone 'd been livin' in it recent like, a lady I guesses. I didn't like to do anything, so I yelled out to Uncle Jack, and he came, and he shot the bolt to bits with his gun. A new fresh bolt, it was, on the outside, and the winders all fixed so no one could get out. And it so 'ot an' all.

"Then Miss Dolly told me, as cool as you like, that her father had taken them from their beds and ridden with them in the bright moonlight until he met this lady, who brought them to the cottage. Dolly told me outright she didn't like this lady, but her father kissed her a lot — I'm sorry, Mrs. Sandford, but that's what she said — before he married her nice mother."

"Tell me the rest, Tom," said Jane, evenly. They were in the ruined drawing-room, which she had taken so much pride in furnishing. Most of the dirt and broken glass had been swept away, and blankets hung over the empty window frames. "Don't be afraid of offending me."

There was not much to Tom's tale. Tom, his shady uncle, and the other, older members of the Wells tribe had held a conference about the best course to take, and it was finally agreed that, seeing the children were so distressed, it would be best to take them back to Miss Fields and Mrs. Sandford at Curwood. Miss Fields, added Tom, almost defiantly, had allus struck him and his mum as havin' her head screwed on right, and everyone knew that young Mrs. Sandford was good-hearted, not a bit like Mr. Sandford.

At this, poor Tom stopped dead. He was not, of course, aware of the real circumstances of Simon's death, and untutored though he was in the social niceties, he knew that he had said something unforgivable to the young widow.

So they both sat in silence for some time. How strange, thought Jane, making this very surprising discovery, Simon was not generally liked. Others could see what I could not, the hard, scheming, avaricious, unscrupulous man behind the romantic looks. There was only one little crumb of comfort in this heartbreaking and tragic affair. Dolly, who had always kept her stepmother at a distance, had told Tom and Jack O'Shea that Jane was the children's nice mother. Poor, confused, unhappy little girl.

"You did right, Tom," she said, at length, "and thank you. What are you going to do? You're very welcome to stay here at Curwood."

"No, thanks all the same, Mrs. Sandford. I promised I'd catch the others up. Uncle Jack's going his own way soon's he can git hisself a decent horse. With them new land laws goin' through so's people like us can git a bit of land of our own, me parents reckon it's time that they looked for somethin' better than the valley."

"Well, stay until morning, and I'll tell Miss Fields to be sure to give you something to eat on the way. Better still, Tom, I'll tell one of the men to take you behind him on horseback so that you catch up quickly. And something else,

302

Tom. As far as I'm concerned, I never saw, thought I saw, nor heard anything about your uncle. And, I'm sure, neither has Miss Fields."

"Just as well you did, Mrs. Sandford. See Uncle Jack, I mean. It got us out of the way of the storm."

Whatever else the Wells family may have been, they were realists.

17

WHEN Tom had gone, James Parker came in, leaner and longer than ever in the flickering candlelight, and shadowed darkly under the eyes from weariness.

"Do you feel able to talk about it?" he asked.

"Yes," she replied, simply. "But, Mr. Parker, you look so very tired. Would *you* prefer to wait?"

"No. Unless you prefer to wait until Whiteside returns tomorrow."

Whiteside, Lily had already told her, had ridden off again, this time to the nearest police station, to report what had happened and to alert them to watch out for Mrs. O'Brien, who, despite her leg injury, had escaped on the horse she had left tethered out of sight. The storm, moving on a narrow front, had, in its capricious fury, dodged Sandford's mistress. (The horse and vehicle in which Jane and Simon had travelled from Curwood were found, unharmed, in exactly the place where they had been left.)

"What Mr. Whiteside and I have to say to each other has nothing to do with . . . Simon."

The tearing grief, the nightmares, the days when time passed by in a grey haze of misery, would come. For the time being, however, Jane was supported by that strength which often comes with shock.

"But before I say more, Mr. Parker, I owe you an apology," she continued, levelly. "From the first, I misjudged you. I even allowed my prejudice against you to destroy my friendship with Chloris McFarlane. What must you have thought of my outburst when we met at Sandhurst?"

His reply was quietly spoken, but emphatic.

"That outburst, Mrs. Sandford, saved your life." Then, having made his point, he went on. "I don't know what my brother-in-law told you about my poor sister, but although the way in which it happened was different, he murdered her

305

as surely as he intended to murder you.

"He was always a greedy, vicious liar. On the surface, he was pleasant enough, and he had a way with women when he put his mind to it. My parents were heartbroken when they discovered that, for the best of reasons, Sally had to marry him. Oh yes, he seduced her, but she wasn't a little slavey in some bush pub. She was Miss Parker of Curwood, and marriage had to follow.

"He had already squandered most of his own inheritance, and except for the gold rush bringing an increased market for meat, he'd have been in Queer Street. After the big fire here in 1851, my parents decided to settle in New Zealand, but I stayed on to try my luck at digging for gold. And I was quite lucky. I invested carefully in town lots, which has helped me to start up in New Zealand. That's the reason I've made so many trips back to Australia — for business purposes, not to concoct a silly scheme of vengeance against Simon."

The candles were flickering badly now. There was a fresher, cooler wind blowing, and the blankets stretched across the empty window frames could not keep out the draught. She arose, to try to fiddle with the makeshift arrangement, but her bandaged hands were too clumsy, and immediately, he came to her aid.

"I'm sorry," he said. "You've already apologised. You were fed so many lies and so much distortion that it wasn't your fault you formed the wrong notion about me."

He continued the story.

"Sally's life became quite wretched. They should have been well off, but he gambled away the profits from his property. Oh, you didn't know? Simon was a gambler."

Jane recollected the letter from the solicitor reprimanding her for spending so much on Curwood, and she knew what should have been obvious at the time. She had not spent nearly as much as he had listed. And how had Simon paid for his right to the Omega run? Lies, her money, or Mrs. O'Brien's?

She said nothing of what was now in her mind, but indicated that the man should keep talking.

"I arrived back from the diggings on a

visit to find Sally in the greatest distress. Simon had formed an association with the wife of a goldfields grog shanty owner. I don't think you'll be surprised, either, when I tell you that the woman was Honora O'Brien. Simon had had other passing interests, but this time, he was deeply involved. They were, it turned out, two of a kind.

"Sally had confronted her husband over his infidelity, and had been beaten for her pains. My friend, Jack Tallence, was with me on this occasion, and rightly or wrongly, an attachment was formed. The saddest part of it was even if Sally had been free, their marriage would have been frowned upon by the less charitable section of our society. Jack's father was English, and his mother was an Indian lady of good family."

Jane gasped, for something else had become clear, the reason why Simon Sandford had so readily accepted fair-haired Rodney as his son.

"Jack, Mrs. Sandford, was the best fellow who ever drew breath, and although he loved Sally very dearly, he knew that his presence nearby would only make things more difficult for her. So, he left the district to prospect in the Gipps Land mountains, I followed him there, and together we were lucky. Then, out of the blue, Sally joined us, bringing little Dolly with her."

"She was desperate. Simon had somehow found out that she cared for another man, and the very fact that Jack was of mixed blood aroused him to a murderous rage. She had no course but to leave him, and I was the only one she could turn to for help. Remember that his sister was married to our elder brother, and at that stage, Lucy sided with Simon. I intended to leave for New Zealand in the near future, and take Sally with me. Simon traced her, however, and although the weather was bitterly cold, he dragged Sally out from our snug little shack, which she shared with *me*, not Jack Tallence. He struck her, and left her lying in the snow, where I found her."

"Oh, be quiet! I can't bear to hear more!"

Jane could feel a dreadful humiliation sweeping through her, filling her with the knowledge that all along she had been, simply, a fool. She put her hands to her ears, trying to blot out what reason told her was the true and rightful version of the tale Simon had recited to her on the night following Inspector Burke's visit.

It was as if she had not spoken. He went on talking, forcing her to listen, and yet, while she rebelled against it, she knew that she needed the truth to help purge her of the horror she had experienced on the flume.

"As I was saying, he took Dolly with him — poor little scrap had a heavy cold and was warmly in her bed, but it was a way of hurting Sally even more. Sally died soon after, as you probably know. Lucy took the baby for the time being, and I went to New Zealand, to stop myself from murdering the swine. Jack returned to India."

What had Aunt Dorcas said, that day on the *Kincardine*, as she and Jane sat over their sewing? Aunt Dorcas' version of the story had been a little embroidered and wrong in some details, but one point had been brutally true. No wife in *that* condition would leave a good husband without reason.

"O'Brien, who had become rich on the proceeds of his goldfields trade, got wind of what was going on between his wife and Sandford, and made it plain that his friends would see to it that Simon would have an accident if he didn't move away. With rumours circulating about Sally's death, Simon decided to sell up and go to England. I might add he was prodded along by Caleb, who'd had enough of him. Simon was soon in financial bother again, and Caleb paid off his debts just to keep him out of the country. Then O'Brien died, and being a shrewd character, he left things arranged so that Honora's income would cease if she remarried.

"Even so, she went off to join her old love, and Caleb decided enough was enough, and wrote to Simon telling him so. This made Simon decide to come back here, for to do him justice, he was very fond of his children, and he knew that Caleb and Lucy would not see them in want.

"I left for New Zealand the day the *Kincardine* berthed, and as Honora was very much in evidence, I was astounded

311

to learn later that Simon had remarried. Lucy and Caleb liked you and were glad that Simon was off their hands financially. Lucy was sure that Simon had come to his senses at last, but Caleb could not believe that Honora O'Brien had taken it all so quietly. Caleb wouldn't be the successful man he is today if he didn't have a gift for sniffing out rats. He quietly found the old duffer of a governess Simon had hired another post and sent along our cousin instead."

"So, Chloris was a spy all along!"

"No, just someone to send out a warning if she noticed anything amiss. But she didn't. Her first letters assured Caleb that Simon seemed to have mended his bad old ways and that you and he were happy together. I must admit that I was more than satisfied at his choice of stepmother for Sally's children."

For the first time, there was the hint of a smile on his face.

"But when we met in Sandhurst, I was stunned by your accusations. Don't you realise, Mrs. Sandford, that the dear friend who died during the Mutiny was

Jack Tallence? I'd had word just before leaving New Zealand. It was impossible that his possessions should have been out in the Whipstick. As for your remark that I'd been spreading rumours about Simon — I'd no need to do that. His own behaviour had caused those rumours, and typically, he'd turned things about so that he appeared to be the victim instead of the villain."

So Simon, seeking an opportunity to set his plans in motion, had used the chance visit of Inspector Burke to create a monstrous fabrication.

"Your accusation prompted me to call on my cousin at Curwood, and Chloris told me an extraordinary story about a letter. Your servant and good friend, Lily, had found the letter which was supposed to come from a dead man, and being no fool, showed it to Chloris, because she was sure that the writing was not Mr. MacBride's. Then there were the spelling mistakes, not typical of Mr. MacBride. Chloris suggested that one person may have drafted out the letter, and another, less well educated, had copied it. Back in Melbourne, I made enquiries, and learnt that Mrs. O'Brien had recently returned from a trip to Sydney.

"Caleb and I were convinced that Simon was up to something, so I stayed quietly in Melbourne, while Caleb let it be known I'd returned to New Zealand. Chloris came back to town, absolutely furious at the way in which she had been blamed for something she had not done, and went instantly to Caleb, fortunately at his place of business, for we did not wish to share our suspicions with poor Lucy. I was sure that our sister had never possessed such a necklace, and went from jeweller to jeweller in Melbourne — hoping that it had not been purchased elsewhere — and eventually found one who had sold a similar trinket to Mrs. O'Brien.

"I was greatly alarmed by now, and did what seemed the proper thing. I went to the police, but all I had was coincidence and suspicion, and I did not receive a good hearing. Then Fate herself stepped in. I was leaving the station in a downcast mood when a man who introduced himself as Evan Whiteside approached me. He had just signed on,

314

but was not due to start his duties until the following week. He had overheard me mention the name Curwood. You could have knocked me down with a feather when he told me that he believed we had an interest in the same lady."

"So," said Jane slowly and grimly, "that is why he came to Australia."

"No, Mrs. Sandford, you were not the reason. His wife's family emigrated a few years ago, and she missed them very badly. Also, ahem, I gather he'd incurred the wrath of a certain prominent citizen back Home because he'd failed to apprehend a culprit who'd dodged justice by dying. Whiteside is a very persistent fellow, and although at first he thought you'd perished in the *Kincardine* disaster, he soon found out that you were alive and married here in Victoria. Then, I knew that there was a sure way of discovering Simon's motives, because Whiteside told me that you weren't entitled to your wealth, and that your father had obtained it for you by a confidence trick."

She began laughing, not the mirth of amusement, but the shrill laughter of semi-hysteria.

"Oh, poor Papa!" she cried out. "In the end, it was he who saved me, not you, nor Mr. Whiteside, nor the storm. It was my Papa!"

Parker brought her a glass of wine, and told her to pull herself together, and after a few moments, she did recover sufficiently to tell him the truth about Papa.

"But I am, truly, the real Jane Terrill," she concluded. "Mr. Whiteside knew me as Jane Turner, but that was an alias. Papa had never intended that I should share his life, and he wrote to my grandfather in New South Wales begging him to give me what was rightly mine, through my mother. Papa received no reply until after my grandfather died, when agents in Britain advertised to seek our whereabouts. There was no fraud there, at least."

It was impossible to tell whether or not he believed her. He said that she would have to discuss the matter with Whiteside, and then passed on to further explanations.

Whiteside had quickly grasped that there was some ground for Parker's suspicions. Within a few hours, he had ferreted out that Mrs. O'Brien was absent from her home, ostensibly visiting friends in Tasmania, although a check of shipping lists did not show her name as one who had recently crossed the straits to that island. This was enough for the two new acquaintances. They came north to Curwood, post haste.

"A stupid plot, and one which was bound to be unravelled in due course," was James Parker's final comment. "But bringing Simon and his lady love to justice would not have given you back your life."

18

TWO years later, Jane could look back on that part of her life with a certain detachment, like someone reading a gothic tale which struck chords, but did not affect one's emotions to any extent.

For a while, there had been much confusion and personal travail. Whiteside was finally convinced that she was indeed the rightful heir to half of her grandfather's estate, and he surprised her greatly when she offered to repay the money her father had swindled in his guise as Pensley Turner.

"Forget about it, Mrs. Sandford," he said, with just the glimmer of a boyish smile. "That party made a fortune out of supplying inferior staff to our troops. I'm an old Crimean man myself, and the money went to the right place. Just you remember this — it's no wonder you were taken in by a blackguard. You'd gotten used to seeing life topsy-turvey."

Other problems were not so easily solved. The worst of these was the long-drawn argument over the guardianship of Simon's children, which began during Mrs. O'Brien's trial for her part in the conspiracy, and continued many months after. To the worry of this wrangle was added the bitterness of seeing Mrs. O'Brien march out of court a free woman, assisted by a shrewd lawyer and an appearance so prim and victimised that not one member of the jury could believe her guilty.

However, this verdict was followed by waspish comments in a press unfettered by the restrictions of a more complicated age, and Mrs. O'Brien removed herself to the United States of America.

For Jane, there was limitless irony in the fact that whilst James Parker gave evidence against Honora at the trial, he and she were at loggerheads. James and Caleb had agreed that the children would be better off in New Zealand, away from the scandal generated by Honora's trial. Jane felt that they had become used to her as a stepmother, and drastic change would be detrimental. Her intention, she argued, to set up house in Sydney in the neighbouring colony of New South Wales meant that they would leave the place associated with their father's death, but have the benefits of continuity with her and faithful Lily Fields in charge.

James Parker returned to New Zealand immediately after the trial, leaving the matter to be fought out between solicitors. His side won. It was pointed out that Mrs. Sandford was still young, and logically, it could be assumed that she would remarry, and there being no blood tie between her and the children, guardianship must pass to their mother's twin.

Jane wept for hours. After all she had suffered, this was too much, and proved that her first impression of James Parker had been correct. She was so furious that if the children had been inanimate objects, she would have packed them into a box and sent them off by the next ship. But, they were living creatures, loving and infuriating, vexing and adorable, by turn. She poured out all her anger and disappointment in a letter to James Parker, concluding emphatically that it was nonsense to suggest that she would remarry, as she had undertaken a vow to avoid matrimony for the rest of her days.

When it was too late, she naturally regretted writing this epistle, and even admitted to herself that Parker could have misgivings about her suitability as a guardian because of Papa's peculiar mode of life. After a few weeks, a strangely mild reply arrived.

As it was not yet convenient for him to undertake the care of the children, his house not being ready and his parents having recently been sick with influenza, it would be well for things to go on as they were. However, he would appreciate regular accounts of the children's progress.

She found a small, but comfortable house in Sydney, with a good view of the harbour and a pretty garden extending right to the water's edge. Except for the constant threat of having the children snatched from her, she would have been content, for she was, after all, still young and resilient with few financial worries. Hugh MacBride's relatives were happy to accept her, and a pleasant social life began to weave itself through her days. Then, without warning, James Parker arrived.

Told by the maid that he had called, she swept out, quite impressive in an absolutely enormous crinoline skirt, ready to do battle, but he was both apologetic and pleasant. He explained that he had come to Sydney without prior notice because he had received urgent word that some good breeding stock for his farm was available.

The visit turned into an unexpectedly pleasant event, with picnics and outings, and two people associating for the first time in an unstrained and normal atmosphere. The children were overjoyed to see their Uncle Jim, but privately to Jane, he admitted that they had best stay with her a little longer. Things were unsettled in New Zealand, he said. There was war again with the Maoris in the north, and although in the South Island they were spared that trouble, many men had joined up and gone off to fight, with the result that work on his property had not gone ahead as he had hoped. His parents, of course, longed to see the children, and anticipated visiting Australia in the near future. She gladly offered her hospitality, and they parted on the friendliest of terms.

After this, correspondence passed back and forth across the Tasman Sea at a great rate. He had some talent for sketching and illustrated his letters with drawings of his new house and views across the plains to the great snow-clad mountains of the South Island. However, on his next visit, two years after Simon's death, he stated firmly that this time he would take the children back with him. His father had not been well, and a visit to Australia was now out of the question.

Jane, who had been building up certain private hopes, stared at him white-faced, tears springing to her eyes, as he reminded her that he was the children's guardian.

"Oh no!" she cried, springing to her feet in alarm. "They think of me as their mother now. And I love them so much. You cannot be so cruel."

For some reason, he turned away before replying, and walked across to the window, as if to admire the view, or to watch Dolly and Rodney as they played boisterously in the garden.

"Rodney needs a man's guidance. He's past the nursery governess stage."

"But Dolly needs her mother."

Too late, she realised the absurdity of her utterance, and stood silent and miserable. Jane was heartbroken and disappointed, for she had thought from the tone of his letters over these past ten months that there had grown up between them a warmth and understanding. She had even convinced herself that what she had taken for coldness was shyness.

"There's a way out of the difficulty, Jane," he said, in a low and solemn voice. "But you must break a vow you once made."

"Vow?" She had no idea what he meant.

"You vowed never to remarry."

She had quite forgotten, and as he came to her, she burst out laughing.

"Oh, Jim," she said, "You must have known how wounded and grieved I was then."

She held out her hands to him, and he took them, and drew her to him, and then, as his mouth pressed down on hers, exploded for all time her belief that he was a cold and unfeeling man.

Later, when she told Lily that she was to marry again, and settle in New Zealand, the other made a little snorting noise, and said that it was high time. All this silly arguing about who was to care for the children, when it had been as plain as the nose on your face that Miss Jane and Mr. Parker were well suited.

Jim was wise enough to understand that my spirit had to heal first, thought Jane.

Then she wondered what Papa would have said. Ah, yes.

"Weeping may endure for a night, but joy cometh in the morning."

THE END

TO FIGHT THE WILD
Rod Ansell and Rachel Percy

Lost in uncharted Australian bush, Rod Ansell survived by hunting and trapping wild animals, improvising shelter and using all the bushman's skills he knew.

COROMANDEL
Pat Barr

India in the 1830s is a hot, uncomfortable place, where the East India Company still rules. Amelia and her new husband find themselves caught up in the animosities which seethe between the old order and the new.

THE SMALL PARTY
Lillian Beckwith

A frightening journey to safety begins for Ruth and her small party as their island is caught up in the dangers of armed insurrection.

THE WILDERNESS WALK
Sheila Bishop

Stifling unpleasant memories of a misbegotten romance in Cleave with Lord Francis Aubrey, Lavinia goes on holiday there with her sister. The two women are thrust into a romantic intrigue involving none other than Lord Francis.

THE RELUCTANT GUEST
Rosalind Brett

Ann Calvert went to spend a month on a South African farm with Theo Borland and his sister. They both proved to be different from her first idea of them, and there was Storr Peterson — the most disturbing man she had ever met.

ONE ENCHANTED SUMMER
Anne Tedlock Brooks

A tale of mystery and romance and a girl who found both during one enchanted summer.

CLOUD OVER MALVERTON
Nancy Buckingham

Dulcie soon realises that something is seriously wrong at Malverton, and when violence strikes she is horrified to find herself under suspicion of murder.

AFTER THOUGHTS
Max Bygraves

The Cockney entertainer tells stories of his East End childhood, of his RAF days, and his post-war showbusiness successes and friendships with fellow comedians.

MOONLIGHT
AND MARCH ROSES
D. Y. Cameron

Lynn's search to trace a missing girl takes her to Spain, where she meets Clive Hendon. While untangling the situation, she untangles her emotions and decides on her own future.